He Was Sprawled Over Most Of The Bed, Including Her Side.

A fierce longing rose within her. She wanted him so much she almost trembled. Closing her eyes, she turned away, willing the strength that had held her in good stead throughout the past year to remain strong enough to endure this morning.

She wished she knew enough to seduce him. Wished she was experienced enough to entice him to make passionate love to her at least once before they split. She'd so like to have one glorious memory to take with her down the long road that stretched out before her if her plan to make him fall in love with her didn't work.

Dear Reader,

Welcome to Silhouette Desire, where you can discover the answers to *all* your romantic questions. Such as...

Q. *What would you think if you discovered the man you love has a secret identity—as a movie star?*

A. That's what happens to the heroine of August's MAN OF THE MONTH, *Don't Fence Me In* by award-winning writer Kathleen Korbel.

Q. *What would you do if you were pregnant, in labor and snowbound with a sexy—but panicked—stranger?*

A. Discover the answer in *Father on the Brink*, the conclusion to Elizabeth Bevarly's FROM HERE TO PATERNITY series.

Q. *Suppose you had to have a marriage of convenience?*

A. Maybe you'd behave like the heroine in Barbara McMahon's *Bride of a Thousand Days*.

Q. *How could you talk a man into fathering your child...no strings attached?*

A. Learn how in Susan Crosby's *Baby Fever!*

Q. *Would you ever marry a stranger?*

A. You might, if he was the hero of Sara Orwig's *The Bride's Choice*.

Q. *What does it take to lasso a sexy cowboy?*

A. Find out in Shawna Delacorte's *Cowboy Dreaming*.

Silhouette Desire...where all your questions are answered and your romantic dreams can come true.

Until next month, happy reading!

Lucia Macro

Senior Editor

Please address questions and book requests to:
Silhouette Reader Service
U.S.: 3010 Walden Ave., P.O. Box 1325, Buffalo, NY 14269
Canadian: P.O. Box 609, Fort Erie, Ont. L2A 5X3

BARBARA McMAHON
BRIDE OF A THOUSAND DAYS

SILHOUETTE *Desire*®

TM ' Published by Silhouette Books
America's Publisher of Contemporary Romance

SILHOUETTE BOOKS

ISBN 0-373-76017-5

BRIDE OF A THOUSAND DAYS

Copyright © 1996 by Barbara McMahon

Printed in U.S.A.

BARBARA McMAHON

was born and raised in the South. She traveled around the world while working for an international airline, then settled down to raise a family and work for a computer firm. She began writing when her children started school. Now that she has been fortunate enough to realize her long-held dream of quitting her "day job" and writing full-time, she and her husband have moved from the San Francisco Bay Area to the Sierra Nevada of California. With the beauty of the mountains visible from her windows, and the pace of life slower, she finds more time than ever to think up stories and share them with others. Barbara also writes for Harlequin Romance. Readers can write to Barbara at P.O. Box 977, Pioneer, CA 95666.

To Sheila, Carol and Barbara
For friendship, ideas and lunches,
Thanks!

Prologue

Cole Langford pulled into the driveway and stopped just behind her car. Slowly he cut the lights and engine and got out. It was twilight, that soft time between day and night when everything was still and the light faded slowly. The old house was dark. He could hear the buzz of the cicadas as they began their nightly song. She had to be home—her car was here.

Slowly he mounted the shallow steps to the wide wooden porch. He wore faded, worn jeans, a dark blue cotton shirt opened at the throat, rolled up at the sleeves, and scuffed running shoes. His expression wavered between bitterness and anger and grim determination. The past year had been hell. He'd lost everything. Lost his wife, his business, his home. For a moment, memories stabbed, hot anger surged through him. He controlled it, clamped down tightly, as he had since he'd first discovered his wife's betrayal. Reaching the front door, he peered through the long oval glass in its center. No glimmer of light showed in the recesses of the house.

He rang the bell. Rang again.

Dammit, she had to be home. Where would she go? Yesterday at the funeral she'd looked so alone. That's when he first caught a glimmer of the idea. He'd thought of nothing else since. Becky had insisted he come by and check on her. So he'd come. And now he'd broach the idea to her. He wasn't sure of her reaction, but he hoped to God she'd agree. With Trisha Anderson's help, he'd be able to pull himself out of the financial morass he'd found himself in and get his life back on track.

He hated depending on anyone. Especially a woman. But the opportunity was too good to let slip by. And it would only be a temporary dependency. Just long enough to solve his problems. If she'd agree to the terms, that is.

Walking around to the back, he spotted her. She was sitting alone on the wooden swing that hung from the overhang of the big back porch. Alone, in the dark. He skirted one of the many islands of flowers in the sea of her green yard and waited for her to notice him. The dahlias and snapdragons and petunias were full of life and vibrant color during the sunny part of the day. Now in the waning light they were an indistinguishable gray. Only their fragrances lingered in the air like a haunting melody. He could smell the honeysuckle that clung to her back fence, the sweet scent reminiscent of the flowers at yesterday's funeral. She'd looked so alone at the grave site. So lost.

"Patricia?"

She looked up. "Cole? What are you doing here?"

Taking the brick stairs to the big back porch, he moved to the swing, sat beside her. She'd been crying. He could see it on her face, in the twisted handkerchief she clutched in her hands. The sundress was rumpled, her feet bare. For a second, something twisted deep within him.

"Came to see how you're doing," he said softly. Without thinking, he reached out and drew her up against him, his arm comforting around her shoulders, his chest something solid for her to lean on.

She relaxed against him and gazed out over the dark yard.

He'd known her for years. She'd been his younger sister Becky's best friend since high school. She was almost like a sister to him. Though he remembered suddenly what a crush she'd had on him when she'd first met him. He smiled without humor; he hadn't thought about that in years. He hoped the tie between their families was strong enough to lend support to his request.

"How're you doing?" His voice was low, soothing.

"I'm okay. Just sad," she said softly. "I'll miss him so much."

"I know. I'm sorry." Her father had been the last of her family. Her mother had died long before they had moved to Norfolk when she'd been sixteen.

"I saw you yesterday, at the funeral. Thanks for coming," she said softly.

He slowly rubbed his fingers against her arm, trying to think of something that would comfort her. Trying to think how to bring up the subject uppermost in his mind without sounding crass and insensitive.

"What are you going to do now?" he asked finally.

Trisha shrugged. "Go on, I guess."

"Did your dad leave you the house?"

"Yes. And I have my job at the library."

"Becky said you'd sold a book. I thought maybe you'd quit the library to write."

"Only one book's been published so far. I'm glad Daddy got to see it. But I don't get any money until after the royalty period is over. And then it will depend on how well it sells. There won't be anything left from his insurance after I pay for the medical expenses and the funeral. I still need my job."

"Plan to be a full-time author one day?" he asked, watching the sky darken to night. The cicadas revved up, their buzz louder as the night grew darker. It was still, hot, humid. Probably wouldn't cool off before morning when the sunrise would assure another hot day in the Tidewater.

"I'd like to, but it'll take a while. I need to support myself in the meantime. I'm almost finished with line edits on another book and will get back to it soon. Just not right now."

The last piece. This was the last piece to make the plan work. It had to. It would benefit them both.

"Trisha, I have an idea I want you to consider," he began hesitantly. It wasn't like him to be so cautious. Suddenly he realized how much he wanted her to say yes. He had to present it properly, to make sure he gave her no reason to refuse. He had to show her how it would benefit them both.

"What?" There was a thread of interest.

"I guess you heard about Diane and me from Becky?" The bitterness was sharp. The anger surged fresh and hot again, though the discovery of his wife's betrayal was over a year old.

"I was sorry to hear you were getting a divorce," she said slowly.

"It's final. Was a couple of weeks ago. Did you also hear I'm flat broke, haven't anything to my name but my clothes?" He tried to keep the bitterness from his tone.

Trisha sat up at that and tried to see him in the darkness. "No! Cole, what happened?"

"Diane went through everything we owned, the savings, the investments. Ran up huge charges on our credit cards before she took off with her lover. It cost me everything to pay the debts. I even had to liquidate the business." For a second the rage threatened to flash out of control. He'd been so stupid, so blind not to see that his wife's compulsive gambling was ruining her, them. By the time he recognized what was going on, it had been too late.

"You had to sell your business?" Trisha said, disbelieving.

"Had to liquidate everything to meet the final settlement. Hell, after all that, I still owe five thousand dollars. And without all the heavy equipment, all the tools and contacts, I can't operate. There are too many other construction firms out there to compete with. I lost it all."

"Oh, Cole, I don't know what to say." She reached out and touched his thigh, wishing to offer some comfort. "How about your dad? He'd love for you to go back into his business with him."

"No. At least not now. I need to prove to him and to myself that I can make it on my own. Besides, one reason I went out on my own to begin with was because his ideas are too old-fashioned for me. We were constantly clashing." He pushed the swing slowly, hoping he could present his plan so she'd accept.

"I may have a way to recoup. But I need some help. Your help if you'd give it to me."

"Of course, you know that. But what can I do? I don't have much money. All we had went for Daddy's last medical expenses."

"I don't need your money. I need you. I've been offered a job with Markham International."

"Working for someone else?" She knew he'd hate it. At least working for his father he'd know one day the business would be his.

"Markham is huge, worldwide, in fact. They've just got the bid for a job in Kuwait, to clean up some of the mess left over from Desert Storm. They're paying top dollar, with bonuses, housing and a living allowance."

"Even so—"

"It's the perfect chance to earn fast money. I figure I can save every penny beyond bare-bone living expenses, most of

which will be furnished by the company. If I go, it'll be for
three years. At the rate they're paying, I'll have enough to
start over when the assignment is finished. More than
enough.''

"Then it sounds as if you should go."

"Yeah, I think so, too. There's only one hitch. Because
of some problems in Kuwait with rambunctious service-
men, Markham is taking no chances with an international
incident. They're only offering jobs to married men and
their wives.''

"Oh no." She was silent for a long moment, then peeked
at him again. "Is there any hope between you and Diane?''

"Not a hope in hell. If I never see her again it will be too
soon for me! But I need a wife.'' He hesitated. He never
thought he'd ask the question again. "Will you marry me,
Trish? Listen, before you say anything, I'll support you entirely. You wouldn't have to do anything but live in the same
house with me. It would be purely platonic. I wouldn't expect husbandly rights or anything like that. The way I feel
about women now, I never want to get entangled again. But
I need this job and the only way to get it is to go over with a
wife.''

"Marry you?" Trisha was astonished. The last thing in
this world she ever expected was for Cole Langford to propose marriage to her.

"In exchange, you could write full-time. Not have any
financial worries while you build that writing career. You
could rent this house, quit your job at the library. By the
time we return, you'll have had time to write several books.
You'll be well established as an author. We'll get a quiet divorce and go our separate ways. I'd give you whatever help
you'd need getting established again. What do you say,
Trisha? Will you help me out?'' He knew from Becky that
Trisha didn't have a special male friend. She rarely dated.
There was nothing to tie her to Norfolk. And he hoped he
made the offer enticing enough that she would accept.

The silence was heavy. Even the cicadas stopped their ceaseless symphony. The stars in the sky sparkled in the velvet night, the wafting scent of honeysuckle filled the dark stillness. Time seemed to stand still as he waited for her answer.

"Yes, Cole, I'll marry you."

One

———

The drone of the airplane should have been soothing, but instead it kept Trisha awake. She gazed out into the inky darkness. Even if it had been bright daylight, there would be nothing to see but the clouds covering the Atlantic. It didn't matter. She stared out into the endless night, wishing she could have held time still.

Everything had happened too suddenly. She had known all along it would end one day. But she had not expected the end to come so soon, so abruptly. She glanced at Cole, asleep beside her. He looked so infinitely dear. His lashes were dark and thick, curling against his cheeks, such a contrast to his sun-bleached blond hair. The lines beside his mouth were relaxed in sleep, not slashingly deep as when he was awake and in tight control.

She turned back to the window, her thoughts chaotic. Over and over the droning of the plane hummed the refrain: *it's over, it's over.*

She'd agreed to be his wife for the three-year tour in Kuwait. Yet their time had been cut short by two years. Was this how Cinderella felt when the clock chimed midnight? Disbelieving, denying, desperate? She longed to turn back time, to start over again. She wished she had the future spread out before her. Instead, suddenly and unexpectedly, it had ended due to his father's heart attack.

She gripped her hands together. It had only been two days since they'd learned of Cole's father's attack and the fact that open-heart surgery was his only chance of long-term survival. When Cole asked for emergency leave from Markham, the company had granted it immediately. They were returning to the United States, the assignment in Kuwait behind them. Trisha didn't believe they would return; there would be too much to do in the United States.

And so their marriage was over.

Tears slowly slid down her cheeks. She brushed them away furtively. She had agreed to the terms. She had known it would end when she started. He wouldn't understand tears. He wouldn't understand how she ached with the thought of the divorce that they'd discussed casually eleven months ago.

And she hadn't fully realized how deeply she loved him. Or how much she would ache living with him and keeping that love hidden. She hadn't expected to hurt this much, knowing their lives together were over and she would be alone for the rest of her life.

"Trish?" Cole drew her hands from her face and turned her slightly. "What's wrong?"

She shook her head. "Nothing." She quickly brushed away the tears. "Just thinking about things."

"Honey, you need to get some sleep. It'll be a long time before we're home. We have customs in New York to get through, and then a three-hour wait for the plane to Norfolk. Come here."

He reclined her seat, pushed up the armrest that separated them and pulled her against his chest, tucking her head beneath his chin. Lightly he brushed his fingertips across her cheek, drying the last of the tears. He held her gently, as a brother might, settling back in his seat.

"Are you worried about my dad?" he asked softly.

She nodded. Let him think the tears were for others. She leaned into his comfort. His hold on her reminded her of the night after her father's funeral. Cole had held her then and it had been wonderful. That had been the night he'd asked her to marry him.

From the time she'd first met him at age sixteen, she'd loved Cole Langford. In the beginning she'd been open with her adoration, but the ridicule she'd found taught her to hide that love and to let it go. He'd never thought of her as more than another sister. She hid her pain when he married Diane, hard as it had been. His marriage had not dimmed her longing to be with him. She always listened avidly whenever Becky spoke of him, wanting to know all she could about every detail of his life, even though he'd long ago moved beyond her reach.

Slowly the steady beat of his heart soothed her. Slowly the strain of the past few days caught up and she began to relax into sleep.

Feeling her soften against him, Cole shifted slightly to get more comfortable, wondering why she'd been crying. He hadn't seen her cry since her father's funeral. Since the night he had proposed. What had caused her tears tonight? Fear for his father? She'd known him a long time. As a teenager she'd always been in and out of their house, almost as at home at his folks' place as Becky. Was she remembering her own father and his final illness?

She should be delighted they were heading Stateside. Happy as a clam that they had left the desert and restrictions behind them. God knew he was glad to be going home. He'd saved every dime he could to repay the last of the debts. That behind him, he'd begun to build a base from which he could operate when he returned home. He could have used the additional income from two more years of work, but he knew his father would need him. At least until he was back on his feet.

It would be good to be back in single-family-home construction. The heavy construction work in Kuwait was not his forte. The money had been good, but the work mindless and boring. And the restrictions in the country had been stifling. Yet he hadn't minded. His goal had been to get free of debt, to rebuild.

How had Trisha viewed it? he wondered for the first time. She never complained. She kept their apartment spotless. Her cooking was even better than his mom's. And she had always seemed so cheerful, no matter how many hardships they'd experienced, like the time the water was off for three days. She'd never once complained. When the power went off with great regularity, she only commented on how hot it got without air-conditioning, but never uttered a word beyond that.

He couldn't have chosen a better partner to live with this past year. Diane would never have made it, even in the early days when he'd thought everything was going well. He'd been smart to ask Trisha. He owed her.

When Cole opened his eyes, dawn glimmered through the plane's windows. Trisha was staring out across the gradually lightening sky. Had she slept for long?

"Are you all right now?" he asked.

She turned back and regarded him with solemn brown eyes. Nodding, she remained silent.

"We should be landing soon," he said, checking his watch.

"It's been a very hectic couple of days," she said, watching him, taking in every delectable inch of the man. From his light sun-streaked hair worn just a trifle long, to the wide expanse of his muscular shoulders, to the long legs sprawled out as much as the seat in front permitted, he personified masculine perfection. She sighed softly, her heart swelling with love for her husband. Her husband in name only.

Sadly she turned to look back out the window. Living with him the past year had been a tightrope walk between heaven and hell. She loved him so much she could scarcely contain it within her. Yet she knew he saw her as no more than a foster sister. Someone to help him out of the financial bind his first wife had caused. She had been very careful to act consistent with the way he saw her, though every instinct urged her to throw herself into his arms and tell him how much she loved him.

"I didn't get a chance to call the Realtor and ask him to give notice to the tenants. I'll have to do that as soon as we get to Norfolk," she murmured absently. Already the tasks ahead seemed insurmountable and inevitable.

"There's no rush."

"Where am I supposed to stay when I get back to Virginia?"

He stared at her for a long moment. "With me," he said slowly. "Where else would you stay?"

"Our agreement was to stay married for the tour of duty in Kuwait. You don't need a wife in the States. You made your position very clear before we married. Check that prenuptial agreement if you've forgotten," she said tightly. It had been a sore point with her. He'd had an attorney draft up a legal document that would have made a saint angry.

"Well, hell, we don't have to divorce the day we reach the States. Good grief, Trisha, you can't think I would turn you out the minute we land. You're like a sister to me. We get on fine. What's the rush?" He frowned at the thought of her returning to her home the day they reached Norfolk. What was her hurry? He knew their marriage was only temporary, but another few weeks or months wouldn't change anything, and it would give her a chance to get used to being on her own again.

"You're the one who didn't want to be married. After Diane, I thought you swore off women forever."

"Yeah, well, that was a long time ago. And I've got enough money saved to start up again on a limited basis. I couldn't have done that without you, honey." His hand brushed against her cheek, brushed again. Had her skin always been so soft? The sweet scent she wore wafted around them, filling the stale airplane air with the fragrance of wildflowers. He would forever associate that scent with Kuwait and Trisha. He felt a tightening low in his belly as he stared down into her warm brown eyes. After all this time, were his feelings toward her changing?

"It was a mutually beneficial agreement, if you'll recall. I couldn't have written as much as I did if I'd still been at the library," she replied fairly.

"Two books in less than a year was pretty good. And just think, once we're home, you can make some of those promotional tours your editor has been requesting."

"I guess. What do you plan to do?"

"We'll stay at Mom and Dad's for a while. Until we see how Dad does in surgery. Then see about getting a place of our own."

"I could give notice to the tenants, we could live in my house," she offered, almost holding her breath. Was he serious about not ending their relationship as soon as possible? Would he consider several months together before he left?

"How much notice do you have to give?"

"A month."

"That might work."

She let her breath out slowly. At least he was agreeable to staying together for another month, and maybe longer.

You're like a sister to me. The words echoed again and again as Trisha stared unseeingly out across the sparkling water far below them. She never wanted to be his sister and she never would be. Maybe, just maybe, it was time she made damn sure he knew exactly that.

She had some time, at least a month while she stayed with him at his parents' place. Could she use that time to make Cole aware of her as a woman, as a possible mate? Make him as aware of her as she was of him? Make him want her the way a man wanted a woman? If he would just give them a chance, they could make a real marriage, share a life together.

But he still saw the betrayal and ruin caused by his first wife. He was blinded to the possible joy of marriage.

Could she change his mind? He said they needn't split when they returned to the States, but she knew he'd be caught up in starting up his own business, finding a place to live. Too busy to fall in love with his wife. She had to act fast if she was ever to have a chance at happily ever after. She had hoped to effect a change during the years in Kuwait, but that was impossible now. And the past year hadn't really made a difference. Would anything have changed in the next two? Time was of the essence. She had one last shot at a lifetime of happiness with the man she loved.

She could do it, or die trying. He'd see she was nothing like Diane. She was no longer going to worry about upsetting the status quo. She'd give it her all. If their marriage ended, it wouldn't be for lack of trying on her part.

And if nothing worked, she had some wonderful memories to sustain her through the future. She wouldn't have traded one day of the past year with Cole for anything. Except to have him notice her as a woman, want her as she wanted him. Love her.

He didn't have a clue. She had never known she was such a good actress, able to hide her feelings for so long. She didn't care to think of what would have happened if she had told him that she loved him as she had been tempted to do on so many occasions. He'd abided by their agreement; the least she could do was the same. But they weren't in Kuwait any longer. And she no longer wished to abide by the terms.

"I never have thanked you for all you've done, Trish. You never complained, you never whined to go home for a visit. You didn't mind that we lived so frugally in order to save money," Cole said as the plane began its descent into JFK Airport.

"I've been happy, Cole. I never lacked for anything. And why would I go home? I have nothing there. Daddy was the last of my family. Besides, I'll consider you part of my family now, brother dear."

He looked startled. His eyes narrowed. "What does that mean?"

She smiled grimly, let him consider that. "You think of me as your sister. I should start thinking of you as the brother I never had." *Like hell, I will. I want you and I'm going to get you,* she promised herself.

He frowned, not liking her comment. It was no more than the truth, but for some reason it bothered him. He was not her brother.

"I need to make a list of all the things we should do," she said primly.

He chuckled, remembering all the times in Kuwait she had whipped out a notebook to jot something down so she wouldn't forget. "You and your lists. You make more than anyone I know."

"I can't keep track of everything if I don't. You know that."

"I know that for the past year you made lists of everything, from groceries to buy, to birthday presents for friends and my family, to which chapter you were going to write and what would go into it. Never saw such a woman for lists," he teased.

She smiled at the shared memories. "Writers get absent-minded when thinking up plots. Lists keep me on track."

She liked his gentle teasing. His eyes grew silver and his face relaxed. So often during the past year he had been worried or remembered the past, falling into a bitter dark mood. She knew when this happened there was nothing to do but wait until his mood passed. Would he ever forget and move on?

Once through customs, Cole found a restaurant, where they ate a hearty breakfast. Wandering around the airport, more to pass time than from any real interest, they finally found the gate for their final leg. Sitting near the door, Trisha drew out her notebook and began jotting down things she needed to do when they were back in Norfolk.

When Cole went to buy a newspaper, Trisha stared at her notebook. She was going to plan her attack and having a list would help her. This was one objective she would not leave to chance. She had a limited opportunity and she needed to make the most of every moment.

She tried to think of what she could do to lure her husband. For the first time she rather wished she'd been a romance writer instead of writing mysteries. Maybe then she'd have bookloads of ideas for seducing a man. She sighed, staring off into space as she tried to plot Cole's downfall.

"I normally sleep naked. I wasn't expecting this," Trisha said, waving a vague hand toward the queen-size bed. Staring at it, she tried to think. It sat oddly amid the mementos of Cole's boyhood room. The trophies, pennants, battered books stacked on the bookshelves and on the scarred desk, displayed interests over a decade old. His mother had changed nothing in his room since he'd moved out. Except for the totally unexpected new bed.

"It's about time we consummated this marriage, don't you think, darling? I'm glad Mom surprised us with the bed. I've wanted you desperately this past year. Don't cover that luscious body of yours."

She glanced up at him, wishing for the millionth time that the dialogue she wrote in her head would actually come from his mouth. God, he was gorgeous! Leaning back against the closed door, he watched her with lazy humor. His arms crossed over his chest, the muscles bulged beneath his cotton shirt. His hair had bleached almost white in the hot Kuwait sun, while his skin had tanned as dark as teak. The combination threw his sparkling gray eyes into prominence. She often felt as if she were drowning in those wonderful cool eyes. She frowned, not liking the amusement she saw. Turning back to her carry-on bag, she rummaged through it, vainly searching for something to wear to bed.

They'd been delayed leaving JFK due to mechanical difficulties, and it had been later than anticipated when they reached Norfolk. She wanted nothing so much as to get to sleep.

"I'm exhausted and you look like you just got up a few minutes ago," she grumbled. Her eyes felt as if they were filled with all the sand on Virginia Beach. Napping on the transatlantic flight had not satisfied her need for sleep. Her body ached with fatigue; it was still on Kuwait time, whatever that was.

"You're cranky because you're tired. What are you trying to do to your clothes, scramble them like eggs?" His voice was calm, soothing.

"I'm looking for something to sleep in. I wasn't expecting to share a bed." Not after all this time. Not after fantasizing about it every night in their apartment in Kuwait. It seemed as if dreams did come true, in a way.

"Let's not bother with clothes, let's just slip beneath the sheets and—"

"I didn't know she bought the bed for us. The last night I slept in this room it had bunk beds," he said patiently. "And with Dad in the hospital, I sure didn't expect Mom to be thinking of us and the bunk beds."

She glanced up. "I'm so tired I can hardly see straight," she murmured, returning to rummaging through her bag to see if she could find something halfway decent to wear to sleep. If she didn't get into bed soon, she'd drop where she stood. Maybe that was the answer. She'd just sleep in her clothes in a puddle beside the bed.

"Here." He tossed a soft white T-shirt across the expanse of mattress. "Wear this tonight and tomorrow we'll see what other arrangement we can make."

She held the shirt up before her; it would easily cover her to the tops of her thighs. For a brief moment she could picture him wearing it. He often left for work wearing a white T-shirt with his soft, faded jeans and tough work boots. Once on the job site, he'd discard the shirt as the sun rose higher and the heat became intolerable. She vividly remembered how his muscular body filled out the shirt the one time she'd visited the site. It would swim on her. Involuntarily she glanced back at the bed. So the shirt would be large. It was better than nothing. And it sure looked as if he wasn't going to use the words she'd hoped he'd say. Not that he ever had, even when she'd fantasized in Kuwait. She sighed. A telepath she was not.

"It's a big bed, Trish, and we're both so tired we won't even know the other is in it. Go to sleep, honey. I'll go down and say good-night to Mom and be up in a little while."

Trisha Langford watched her husband of eleven months leave the bedroom. "Maybe you won't know I'm in it, but I'll sure know you're there," she said softly after the door clicked behind him. If she weren't so tired, she'd appreciate the irony of the situation. For over a decade she'd wanted to sleep with Cole. And for most of that time he hadn't even been aware of her, or only saw her as his sister's friend. Be careful what you wish for, went the old saying. Now she knew why. The reality was not at all the way she wanted.

She drew the T-shirt up to her face, rubbing it gently against her cheek. It smelled of outdoors and soap. Was there a hint of his scent? God, she had it bad. Moving her suitcase, she quickly stripped down and donned the soft cotton shirt. It flowed over her skin like a caress. She smiled, knowing it covered Cole like a second skin. For a moment she almost imagined warmth from his body.

Slipping beneath the sheet, she switched off the bedside light, leaving on the one by his side. Her body ached she was so tired. It wasn't easy traveling from Kuwait to Virginia all in one day. Especially with the uncertainty and worry they faced because of Cole's father's unexpected heart attack. And the worry about her own future. Tomorrow there would be so much to deal with. But for now she relished the soft mattress, the clean sheets... In only seconds Trisha fell sound asleep.

Slowly, consciousness seeped in. Heat enveloped her. Damn, wasn't the air conditioner working again? The reliability of the electricity in Kuwait left much to be desired. You'd think that a country that had so much oil—

Her eyes flew open. She wasn't in Kuwait any longer. She was home. Or rather, back in Virginia. But it was still hot.

She shifted slightly, hitting the hard muscles behind her, feeling a heavy weight across her waist. Slowly she turned. Cole lay right beside her, his hand beneath the hem of her shirt, resting on the bare skin of her belly, his arm heavy across her waist. It was his body heat that woke her, enveloped her.

For a long moment Trisha held her breath. Sliding and turning until she lay flat on her back, she studied him.

He was sound asleep, his breathing deep and even. Tracing his much-loved features gently with her eyes, she stored the memory. Her only time sleeping with her husband. She wouldn't forget a single thing, from his tousled and mussed sun-streaked hair to his dark lashes lying like shadow crescents against his tanned cheeks; from the stubborn chin to his arched eyebrows. The rough stubble of his beard beckoned. She longed to run her fingertips across his jaw, feel the slight abrasion she knew she'd find.

He looked even bigger in bed than when standing. Or maybe he seemed bigger because he was so close to her. His hand rested against her, hot, heavy, tantalizing. He'd slipped it beneath the shirt she wore and his palm felt like a brand against her bare skin. He was sprawled over most of the bed, including her side.

A fierce longing rose within her. She wanted him so much she almost trembled. Closing her eyes, she turned away, willing the strength that had held her in good stead throughout the past year to remain strong enough to endure this morning. She wished she knew enough to seduce him. Wished she was experienced enough to entice him to make passionate love to her at least once before they split. She'd so like to have one glorious memory to take with her down the long, lonely road that stretched out before her if her plan to make him fall in love with her didn't work.

When would he tell her goodbye? She'd done as he'd asked, married him so he could work in Kuwait. While the time wasn't officially over, their assignment in Kuwait had ended. She knew they were back in Virginia for good. Their marriage was no longer needed.

She sighed, pressing her palm against her breast as if that could assuage the ache that spread. She had cherished every moment together. She thought she would have more, thought she would have three full years.

"Awake?" His voice was a low murmur in her ear, his breath a gentle breeze against her cheek.

Spinning back, she gazed into his deep gray eyes. Flushing with the close proximity, with the intensity of feeling she always experienced around him, she nodded shyly. She wished her heart didn't catch every time he looked at her. Wished after all these years she could ignore the tingling sensation being near him always brought. Wished she saw him as no more than her friend Becky's older brother.

"Sleep enough?" he asked, his eyes lazy in the early morning, his body still relaxed.

"I guess." Her heartbeat increased. His solid presence only inches from her disturbed her, his hand resting hot on her belly sent shivering waves of sensation that splashed through her as they heated her blood. Did he realize he touched her so intimately? She wished she dared move beneath his hand, push it up—

"What time is it?" she asked almost desperately.

He shrugged. "I don't know and don't want to move to see the clock. Not too early, the sun's well up."

"What time are you going to the hospital?" She couldn't believe they were having an ordinary conversation while they were lying in bed, she wearing only a T-shirt. Had Cole worn anything? His chest was bare, the sheet stopping at his waist. Curiosity became a raging need. Was he wearing anything at all beneath the sheet?

"Mom said visiting hours start at eleven. We can go then."

"You want me to go, too?"

"Of course." He frowned. "You're my wife. Dad'll want to see you, too. Don't you want to go?"

"Yes. I just wasn't sure."

Even now the memory of the evening after her father's funeral was vividly etched in her mind, every detail as clear as if it had happened yesterday. "I guess I thought since we would end the marriage now that we're back, you wouldn't want to keep up the pretense of a happy marriage. We won't be returning to Kuwait, will we?"

He shook his head. "I doubt it. I'll know more after we see Dad and I can judge how things stand with the business. We agreed last year to give the appearance of a normal marriage to stop any questions. I want to continue now. I told you yesterday we didn't need to separate just because we've returned home."

"No?"

"Not yet, anyway. Trish, you saw my mother last night. She's a nervous wreck. She's always depended so much on Dad. Now she's going to need us until he's well again. And I don't think Dad needs any more upsets until he's recovered. They think this marriage is solid. I don't want to change that yet."

"And our separating would be upsetting?" It made sense. The Langfords had been delighted when Cole had announced their marriage. She had practically been a part of their family since she was a teenager. They had welcomed her even more fervently in light of Cole's disastrous first marriage. They would be disappointed when he divorced her. Though she wished he wanted to stay married for different reasons.

"Damn straight. You remember how ecstatic they were when we married. A lot more enthusiastic than they ever were with Diane. I certainly don't want to do anything now to jeopardize Dad's health, or Mom's mental state. We stay married until he's well again."

"That could be a couple of months," she said slowly, impatient with his arrogance. What if she didn't want to stay married any longer? The bargain had been while they were in Kuwait. How like him to assume she'd do his bidding, just because she had always done so.

"Or even longer. Don't worry, we'll keep the same arrangement. I'll support you, you work on your writing."

The same arrangement? What about sharing a bed?

"I'm starting to make some money with the books now so I don't need your support—"

"Don't argue. I told you I would support you while we were married. When we split, you'll need that money. You won't be getting anything else from me. That was our bargain." His voice grew cold, his eyes icy.

"Except help to get reestablished, remember?" she said, hurt afresh by his reminder of their agreement. She grew more and more tired of reaping the results of Diane's sowing.

"Yes. Just how much will that cost me?" he asked cynically.

"I've thought about it. I won't need money from you. I have my house. I'll give the tenants notice right away and be able to move back in by the time your father's well."

"You've thought it all out, have you?" He frowned. Why he didn't like hearing that, he wasn't sure. It was what they'd agreed to last summer. The timetable had just moved up a bit. Instead of three years, now it would be sooner. He should be delighted she wasn't going to try to soak him for money. He knew Trisha would never create a scene the way Diane would have. But he didn't like talking about ending things between them, either. They had gotten on well during the months in Kuwait. He liked coming home to Trisha, telling her a bit about work, eating the meals she always had ready. True, they no longer needed the marriage, but there would be time enough later to discuss ending it.

"I will need some help, however," she said hesitantly, glancing at him from beneath lowered lashes. This was it. If he showed no reaction, or if he eagerly agreed, she'd know she hadn't a chance.

"Whatever you need, let me know."

"Dating."

"What?" It was the last thing he'd expected to hear.

"Dating. You know, how to play the game. How to offer scintillating conversation. How to get someone interested in me. Basic instruction in how to entice a man."

Two

Cole rose up on one elbow, leaned over her, his eyes hard. "What the hell are you talking about?"

Trisha met his gaze fearlessly, secretly intrigued that he showed so much reaction. "I'm talking about you teaching me how to attract a man. During this past year I discovered I like being married. Only next time I want to share the bedroom, as well. I don't want another platonic relationship. I didn't date much when I was younger." No need to let him know she had always hoped he would ask her out. And the dates she had gone on had not proved very successful because she compared every man to Cole. "The past couple of years I spent tied up with my dad because he was so sick, or with you. So I'm way out of practice."

"We're sharing a bed now," he muttered, still glaring down at her. He wasn't some adviser to the lovelorn. And he damn sure didn't like her talk about getting in bed with another man. She was still married to him and had better remember that! If she didn't want a platonic relationship, all she had to do was tell him.

"Cole," she said gently, firmly removing his hand from her body before she threw herself into his arms and begged him to make love to her. "I've done all you asked in this marriage. I'll even stay married a little longer, even though we're no longer in Kuwait, in order to help you out with your folks. But you said you'd help me when we split. You promised. I've decided I like being married, being part of a couple. I'm calling in your marker. You have to help me find a husband."

"Damn!" He lay back and stared at the ceiling. His quiet, shy little librarian-turned-author wife had just shocked the hell out of him. Trisha had always seemed so content working at the library, living with her dad. He knew from Becky that Trisha didn't date much. He'd never had to envision her with a man. She'd been the perfect wife during their time in Kuwait, always cheerful, always ready to do whatever he wanted, from last-minute dinners for fellow construction workers to accommodating his long, irregular hours. She hadn't asked for much. Until now. Now she expected his help in finding her a husband.

If he wasn't so against marriage, he'd stay married to her himself. She was fun to be around, easy to talk to and could cook like a dream. Closing his eyes, he swore again softly. That had to be the most foolish idea he'd ever come up with. He was through with marriage. He refused to get tangled up with another woman and risk losing everything a second time. They'd made their agreement. And he had promised to help her. So he would, if that was what she really wanted. *Dammit to hell!*

"I'll take a quick shower and then you can have the bathroom," Trisha said, taking advantage of Cole's silence. She hastened across the hallway and closed the bathroom door behind her, leaning against it for a long moment. She felt almost giddy with relief and surging hope. Many more seconds in close proximity with him like that and she'd become a babbling fool. God, he was so clueless. She had loved him for over a decade, since the first time she'd seen him when she'd come over to visit Becky after moving into the neighborhood. And he hadn't an inkling.

Turning on the shower, she tried to think of more mundane things. Reveling in the warm water that cascaded over her, she plunged gleefully beneath the strong shower. The amenities in Kuwait had been less than first-class. She let the water soothe her. She needed the relaxation to spark her creativity. Once again she wished she had tried romance writing instead of mysteries. She knew forty-three ways to poison someone without leaving a trace, but hadn't a clue how to seduce one stubborn, arrogant, sexy man who was determined that all women were out to get him.

Win or lose, she was determined to make Cole Langford see her as a desirable woman at least once before they separated. Maybe he could point out what he liked in a woman, while ostensibly trying to help her find a new husband. She could adjust herself to his needs. One night—that's all she asked. Was it too much? She'd resigned herself to being alone years ago. Knowing he saw her as a sister, she knew he'd never fall passionately, lastingly in love with her. But she'd so much like to have one special night before they separated.

Yeah, and maybe pigs would fly.

It was worth a try, she argued. She had nothing to lose. If she didn't do something, and soon, she would find herself divorced and alone again. Knowing Cole, he'd never have asked her to marry him if he hadn't needed a wife in Kuwait. Once single again, she doubted he ever would remarry. She'd hoped being the perfect wife in Kuwait would demonstrate that he needed her in his life.

But he had been too caught up in work to even notice her. As soon as his father was on the road to recovery, Cole would stick to the original plan to end their marriage. The only reason to delay was, it was more convenient for him to wait until his father was well. It didn't matter; she had gained a reprieve. Time to change tactics. Obviously the ones she'd tried up to now hadn't worked. She still had a few weeks. She was determined to seduce that sexy man or die trying.

Finished with her shower, Trisha dried herself off and pulled on the T-shirt. Wrapping a fresh towel like a turban around her long wet hair, she slipped back across the hall into their bedroom.

After a year of separate bedrooms, to be expected to share one had startled her last night. Now, just maybe it would turn out to be the best thing. Especially since she planned to start her new campaign immediately.

Cole leaned back against the headboard when she returned, his gaze running down her body, his expression unreadable as he studied her. She tried to ignore the flash of heat that burst deep inside and treat their situation as normally as she could. Was she actress enough?

"The bathroom's all yours," she said easily, going to her suitcase and rummaging around again, looking for clean underwear and the dress she'd wear today. It would have to be ironed. After being packed for two days, everything in the suitcase would be wrinkled beyond belief.

"Thanks." Cole found he didn't want to leave. He wanted to stay and see if she'd get dressed in front of him. He wanted to snatch away that towel and see her blond hair settle over her shoulders, wet and straight. He knew it would dry soft and wavy. His hands ached to push up his T-shirt that covered her so enticingly and touch the honey sweetness of her skin. She appeared so self-contained, so self-assured, it angered him. He'd like to rattle her a bit, shake her up the way she'd shaken him up with her request that he help her find a husband. After all these years he thought he knew Trisha, but was beginning to discover he hadn't a clue. Was she as devious as Diane had been? Was he going to find the quiet malleable woman he'd married had a different agenda? For a moment the old bitterness rose. Damn if he'd let her or any woman manipulate him again. When his dad recovered, they'd separate, get a divorce. They'd agreed to do that a year ago and he'd make sure they followed through.

Only…he didn't like the final terms, that he help her find another man. He wondered if she'd ever made love before. If she would be as sweet and generous in bed as she had been this past year living in the heat and hardships of Kuwait. Once or twice in Kuwait he'd wondered the same thing. But he'd honored the terms of their agreement. Now she was proposing to find another man. Sleep with him. Cole didn't like the situation at all.

Rising reluctantly, he drew on his jeans and hunted for clothes to wear after his shower. Normally he also slept in the nude, but had worn briefs last night out of consideration for Trisha. He smiled grimly. That had been another shock, to discover his prim, shy wife normally slept in the raw. He'd like to cuddle up with her, feel her honey heat against his skin. Strip that cotton shirt from her and lie with her, touching from top to toe.

Without another word, he slammed out of the bedroom and headed for the bathroom. God, after living with her for a year, was he now starting to desire his wife? His timing stank.

In seconds he returned. He'd forgotten his shaving kit. He was lucky he could remember his way to the bathroom after her shocking announcement. He wanted to stay and—

He stopped, poleaxed. Desire hit Cole low down, hot and hard. He stared at her. They'd been married almost a year and this was the first time he'd seen her undressed.

Quickly he scanned her slender frame. She was incredibly lovely. Why hadn't he noticed before now? Trisha had donned a brief pair of French-cut bikini panties that accentuated her long, tanned legs. The lace revealed more than it concealed as blond curls peeked out. The skimpy covering was a shock; he would have expected plain white cotton briefs.

She paused momentarily when he burst back into the room, then resumed pulling on a matching bra. The wild lavender color complemented her honey-gold skin. But the firm breasts still waiting to be confined caught his eye and wouldn't let go. Her nipples were rosy and slightly puckered. The smooth globes of her breasts were high and firm and stained a pale pink with her embarrassment. Cole couldn't look away. Even covered with the pale lace and satin, he wanted to touch them, feel their weight in his palms, taste their sweetness in his mouth. Stunned at the reaction in his gut, he raised his gaze to clash with Trisha's.

Trisha fastened her bra while holding Cole's gaze. Her heart pounded as she fought for control. With an insouciance she was far from feeling, she slowly drew the towel from around her hair, then shook the strands free. Her heart was pumping as if she'd just run a race. She could feel his eyes on her like a hot brand. Determined to ignore the shivering sensations that shook her, she took a deep breath and willed her voice to come out normal.

"Does your mother have an iron I can use?" she said. If he didn't stop looking at her like he was going to eat her up, she'd melt down right where she stood. Heat licked through her. She wanted to throw herself against him. But she held her ground, tilting her chin slightly, fighting the urge to cover herself. Maybe this was exactly the kind of thing he needed to wake up to the fact she was a woman. One who wanted him.

"God, Trisha, I never knew you were so lovely, so beautiful all over. Just let me feast my eyes on your beauty. Oh, my love, I want you so badly."

"Yeah, sure. Mom has one in the laundry room. I'll get it." His eyes ran down her slim figure. He remembered the feel of her warm skin against his palm when he awoke. He wanted to feel her skin all over, run his roughened hand over every inch of her. Her hips were softly rounded, her legs long and tanned. The shadow between her breasts drew his gaze again.

God, he had to get out of here before he forgot all about going to the hospital, forgot about his mother's need for support and tossed Trisha on their rumpled bed and kissed her senseless.

Then made love to her all day long.

"Thanks," she replied sweetly, smiling at him.

Her voice was breathless and something about it inflamed him. Her eyes glittered softly in the morning light as she flickered them his way, then ignored him as she finished fastening the bra. She was so pretty. Was he only realizing that now? She wouldn't have any trouble finding a man. Jealousy flared. Frowning, Cole turned away. He'd get the blasted iron, then take a shower. A cold shower.

Trisha watched him leave, disappointed once again that he'd not said the words she'd so wanted him to say. Sighing softly, she turned to make the bed. Even standing almost naked before him had had no effect. Scrap a striptease to tantalize him—obviously that didn't have the slightest impact. Was there anything she could do that would?

Cole returned with an iron and ironing board. He seemed angry. Trisha thanked him and watched as he slammed their door behind him. Two seconds later he opened it again and stormed over to his suitcase and snatched up his shaving kit. Without looking at her, he left, slamming the door behind him a second time.

Slowly she began to smile. Maybe, just maybe, there had been some effect.

By the time they were ready to leave for the hospital, Trisha had thought through various steps she would take to make this husband of hers sit up and take notice. She had jotted them down on her ever-present notepad. She would have to fine-tune the plan, but it was a start.

First she needed to show him all the things she could do to make herself indispensable to his family, show him she was as different from Diane as night was from day. Second, she needed to show him she didn't need him for money. Her first book had sold extremely well. Her second two were already out and her publisher expected even higher sales.

Not that Cole had ever shown an interest in her writing, beyond inquiring how the day-to-day work at the computer had gone. He'd be surprised at her success, and maybe it would change his mind about her. She certainly wasn't a gambler the way Diane had been. She didn't have a lover on the side. Sighing softly, she hated to admit she didn't have a lover anywhere. Cole could change that. Would he?

She paused at the kitchen door. She wasn't going to bribe him. She would get him to acknowledge an attraction between them before telling him of her success. She needed to make sure he cared for her. If only a little bit.

He had to. She had loved him for so long she couldn't stand it if he didn't even care slightly for her. She'd been truthful when she'd told him she liked being married—but only to him. Would he let her go? Would he help her get back into dating? If so, her case was hopeless. She could only wait and see what Cole did.

Matt Langford was still in the cardiac care unit and permitted only one visitor at a time and only for a few minutes. His wife went to see him when the three of them arrived at the hospital. Cole and Trisha sat in the waiting area. The room had a large window that overlooked the hospital grounds. The chairs and sofas were standard institutional issue. Still, the room was comfortable.

"This must be hard for you," Cole said as he sat on one of the sofas, facing the window, remembering Trisha's father had been in this same hospital when he died.

She nodded, saying nothing, grateful to sit down. Old memories had surfaced. She remembered being here just a year ago. Only her father had been too sick to recover. She hoped the outcome would be different for Cole's dad.

When he reached over to take her cold hand, she looked at him, startled by his touch. She didn't think he'd touched her more than a couple of times during their entire stay in Kuwait. But since hearing about his father, he'd held her on the plane, held her last night, and now this.

"Come here, sit beside me." He scooted over on the small sofa and drew her out of the chair to sit beside him. Lacing his fingers with hers, he rested their linked hands on his hard thigh.

"I'm sure your father will be all right," she said, wanting to comfort him, confused by his touch. He'd never held hands with her before, especially not in such an intimate fashion.

"I guess. We'll have more information after we talk to his doctor. Mom said he felt Dad was as strong as he was going to get for the surgery. They don't want to delay any longer. I feel so helpless, like I ought to be able to do something. What if he doesn't recover, Trish? He's not an old man, only fifty-eight."

"Your mom said he'd been in bad health for quite some time."

"So she said, but he hid it. Which is just like him, I guess. He always was a strong man. I always thought of him as invincible."

"Then this illness will prove hard for him. He'll need you around even more than your mom does, I think," Trisha said. "You'll have to run the business while he's recovering. He trusts you and won't worry if you're in charge. You know it's going to take him a long time to get better."

Cole eyed her oddly. "You expect me to step in and run my father's business?"

"Who else?" She shrugged. "Someone has to do it. You worked with him before you went out on your own. He never wanted you to go, you know. He always wanted it to be Langford and Son. He'll leave it to you one day."

"Think so?" His voice cooled noticeably.

She nodded, puzzled by his tone. "Of course. You must know it, too. Good heavens, Cole, you worked for him every summer through high school and college. Started out with him when you got your engineering degree. You know he always wanted you in business with him."

"He and I lasted less than a year when I worked full-time for him. He wants to do large tracts of houses, condos or fancy apartments. I want to do custom homes, put a lot of craftsmanship into them, make them distinctive and unique. We never agreed on anything when I worked for him."

She shrugged. "It won't matter now. You'll be in charge until he's back. Time enough then to see if you want to stay with him or go off on your own again. But my guess is that he'll want you to stay, maybe make you a full partner."

"If he did, I'd be set again. I wouldn't have to worry about starting over, wouldn't have to work my way back up. But I'd need someone with me, to help me. You, Trisha, I need you. Please say you'll stay with me. Forget our plans for a divorce. Be my wife."

"You'd like that, wouldn't you? It would mean instant success, instant wealth. But don't forget our bargain—you get nothing when we split." His voice was cool, remote.

She started as if he'd slapped her. Yanking her hand free of his, she rose and turned to glare at him, hands on her hips, leaning over him to make sure he could look no farther than her face.

"Listen to me, you arrogant idiot, I don't want anything from you!" *Except your love, which you won't ever give.* "It must be extremely difficult to think the whole female population is against you. Well, I've got news for you, buster, this is one female who will count herself lucky when this farce of a marriage is over. Of all the opinionated, self-centered, dumb males I've ever known, you take the cake.

Yes, you got a raw deal with Diane, but not all women are like Diane. But you just go ahead and wallow in that self-pity you love so much and ignore everyone who might genuinely be interested in you, who might want to help you.''

"What? No protestations of undying love? You weren't so reticent as a teenager. I practically had to beat you off with a stick,'' he retorted, stung by her words.

She stood upright, knowing the color drained from her face. How nasty of him to remind her of her crush when she'd first met him. She knew she'd been blatantly chasing him, but she'd only been sixteen. She'd taken great pains to hide her feelings from him once she'd overheard him laughing about her with some of his buddies. She'd been crushed. She couldn't help loving the man, but she sure as hell didn't have to let him know it. Tilting her chin, she glared at him.

"That was a long time ago, Cole. You should be so lucky to have me love you now.'' With that she turned and stalked away. She'd wait in the hall outside Matt's room for her turn to visit, then leave and check on the situation with her house. For the first time in hours the thought of making love with Cole was not uppermost in her mind. In fact, she wondered how she could continue to love him when he was so impossible.

Cole rubbed his face as he watched her storm away. Damn, he hadn't meant to insult her. He must be suffering from jet lag. Was that her excuse? How dare she talk to him like that. What was the matter with her? Ever since they'd arrived last night Trisha had changed. Gone was the quiet, shy woman he'd known for years. Instead, he was being treated to a tempting, sexy female who had no qualms about making herself and her feelings known. Which was the real Trisha? The quiet friend of his sister he'd lived with this past year, or the hotheaded, provocative woman of this morning?

It must be jet lag.

He shouldn't have made the crack about her crush on him as a teenager. Truth to tell, at the time he'd been flattered. She'd been a pretty girl even then. But she was his younger sister's friend, and he hadn't wanted to be razzed by his buddies, so he'd laughed it away. After a few months, she'd stayed away. She'd stopped coming after him, had virtually ignored him in the years that had followed.

She hadn't even come to his wedding to Diane, though she and her father had been invited. He wondered why. Not that it mattered, and thinking about Diane put him in a bad mood. If she hadn't been such a compulsive gambler, hiding the fact before their marriage, discounting its importance in her life after their wedding, he'd not be in the financial situation he was in today.

And if she hadn't been such a cheat, he might still be married to her. But she'd taken off with a man who had much more wealth than she would ever see with Cole. Idly he wondered if she had run through the new man's money yet.

Why hadn't he expected problems with Diane? He'd had enough problems before when dealing with the opposite sex. From Sara in high school to Bonnie in college to Diane, his track record was appalling. From experience he knew Trisha would be no different. She only wanted him for her own gain. If he hadn't offered to support her to build her writing career, she wouldn't have married him. For all her fancy talk, that was the bottom line.

Cole shifted his gaze out the window, thinking about what he and Trisha had discussed. Would his father want Cole to assume control of Langford Construction until he recovered? What if he never recovered sufficiently to return to the helm? For a long, dark moment Cole considered the various ramifications. He wanted his father's full recovery. Business was secondary. He could run Langford Construction, but he'd want to make changes. He would finish out the contracts they now had, but if his father wasn't ready to return to work by then, Cole would like to expand into the custom home market. Maybe do both custom work and the cookie-cutter developments his father preferred.

He must be getting older; now he was thinking compromise. He smiled grimly and shook his head. What would Trisha think? He quickly pushed the thought from his mind. She wouldn't be part of his life after the next few weeks. Or only as a family friend. It didn't matter what she thought.

For one brief second he hoped his father would take months to recover. That would mean that Trisha would stay around, and they could live as they had in Kuwait. No sense rushing to separate. Besides, he wasn't ready to have her dating again. Plenty of time for that in the future.

Trisha spent her allotted five minutes with her father-in-law. Secretly appalled at how bad he looked, with all the tubes and wires connecting him to various machines, she gave a good performance of how pleased she was to see him, and how glad she was to be home. Fortunately, there wasn't much time to talk and she escaped gladly, lest she give something away to indicate that everything wasn't going as well in her marriage as the older Langfords thought.

"Trisha?"

"Becky! Oh, I'm so glad to see you!" Trisha flung her arms around her longtime friend and hugged her hard. "I'm so sorry about your dad, but he seems in good spirits and that's the important thing. I'm sure he'll come through the surgery with flying colors."

"I hope so. It's been so hard. I'm so glad you and Cole came back. Where is he, in with Dad?" Becky wasn't as tall as Trisha, and had hair a shade darker than her brother's. She was also seven months pregnant.

"No, he's in the waiting room. I just finished my visit with your dad. We're doing it one at a time, you know. Your mom went first, of course. Did you want to see him now?"

"Let Cole visit first. Tell me everything. Your letters have been sporadic, at best. I thought you were a writer." Linking arms with her best friend, Becky headed toward the small waiting room.

Trisha smiled. "By the time I finished working on my book every day, I was too tired to think about writing a letter. Besides, life in Kuwait was so routine you knew everything we did after my first letter."

"Cole!" Becky rushed over to hug her brother when they reached the waiting room. "Your turn to see Dad. I'll visit when you're done. It's good to have you back."

"Good to see you, Becky. How are Tom and the boys? Were you as large with the last two as this one?" he asked, giving her a quick hug.

She grinned. "Yep. Tom and the boys are fine. You have to see Tyler. He's grown so much you won't recognize him. And Trevor's in preschool." Slyly she glanced around at Trisha. "Any interesting announcements you two would like to make? All in the family, so to speak?"

Trisha smiled and shook her head, hoping the ache in her heart didn't reflect in her expression. She would love to have a child with Cole. Being an only child herself, she had always longed to have a large family. Now that her father and mother were both gone, she wished for a family even more than ever. Another foolish dream that would never come true. She wanted to be the mother of Cole's children, and he was planning a divorce.

Cole answered briskly as he headed toward his father's room. "No, we're not planning a family. I'll talk to you after I see Dad."

Becky watched him walk away with surprise, then swung her gaze to Trisha.

"Never?"

Trisha shrugged and went to sit down. She didn't want to have to meet Becky's eyes. "Did you bring pictures of the boys? I can't believe Tyler is over two."

"Well, I just happen to have a couple of recent pictures." Becky sat down beside Trisha and eagerly opened her purse. In only seconds they were bent over the pictures of Becky's boys.

Trisha gazed at them longingly. She yearned to have a little boy. Or a little girl. It didn't matter, as long as it was Cole's baby. Sighing softly, her determination grew stronger. She so wanted to prove to her stubborn husband that she would make him an excellent wife, and not just until his father recovered, but forever. He deserved some happiness after the heartache Diane had put him through. Together they deserved a nice family and she wondered what she could do to give them a chance. Being the perfect wife in Kuwait had not been enough. Would the intimacy of sharing a room make a difference?

"That's enough about my kids. You and Cole will have to come over in a couple of days and see them. And Tom. But tell me about your writing. We were so thrilled when *Open the Gate to Death* hit the bestseller list. That was unexpected, wasn't it?"

"Yes. Especially for a first book. My publisher did a grand job with publicity."

"Nonsense. You did a great job writing the book. I loved it, and *Killer Instinct*. Wasn't that one on the bestseller list for weeks and weeks? I've already purchased *Mocking Death Again*. I told the bookstore near us to call me the day it came in, which was yesterday. I haven't had a chance to read it yet, but I've got one of the first ones in the entire area."

Trisha smiled at her friend. "I'm so honored. You didn't have to buy it—I would have given you one, silly."

"No, I want to help establish your bestselling records. What does Cole think of all this?"

"Actually, he doesn't, um, know about it. He was so busy in Kuwait. The project turned out to be very demanding..." Trisha trailed off. It was hard to explain exactly why she hadn't shared every triumph with him. It had been tied up with the reason for their agreement and Trisha's not wanting him to think she was bragging or trying to entice him through bribery with her success. And she knew he blamed himself for the financial situation Diane had caused. It was startling how much money she'd made on her first book. And the advance on the next two had been staggering. Somehow she'd thought it would make him feel differently toward her and she hadn't wanted to risk it.

And it had been so easy to keep silent in Kuwait. He never asked and they weren't surrounded by people who mentioned her books. Now she wasn't so sure keeping quiet had been a good idea. She should tell him. Trisha didn't want him to hear about it secondhand. Which he might, especially if Becky set herself up to be a one-woman cheering section.

Becky stared at her in astonishment. "How busy is too busy? What did that have to do with anything? It would only take five seconds to say 'my book hit the *New York Times* bestseller list.' "

Trisha shrugged, wishing she'd anticipated this. If Becky knew what her agent was working on now, she'd go through the roof. And she was right, Trisha did need to let her husband know, and soon, before Becky spilled it. "It wasn't so important over in Kuwait. I'll tell him."

"How can you say it wasn't important? Good grief, girl, the *New York Times* bestseller list! Just when were you planning to tell him?" Becky demanded.

Trisha smiled, remembering how Becky always liked things done instantly. "Soon."

Becky stared at her strangely. "You know," she said slowly, "I've often wondered over the past year what happened between you and Cole that caused you to get married so quickly. He seemed so bitter after the divorce with Diane. Then your father died, and the next thing I knew, you two were married and moving to Kuwait."

"It wasn't that sudden. You came to the wedding."

Becky shook her head. "If you could call it that. A hurried affair at the courthouse. I remember you always dreamed about a large wedding, with all our friends and a beautiful dress."

"I know, but when Daddy died, I didn't feel the same," Trisha said. She would have loved a big wedding, but without her father, the dream had lost some of its luster. And of course their marriage was only a business arrangement. She sighed. Life took funny turns.

Three

———

Cole came out of his father's room and leaned against the wall, staring at the ceiling as if for answers. Damn, his dad looked worse than he'd expected. He needed to talk to the doctor and get a realistic assessment of the probability of his father's recovery. He wanted an estimated length of time for his convalescence. Cole wasn't at all sure his dad would be back at work as soon as he thought.

It looked as if Trisha's assessment was on the mark. He'd be heading up Langford Construction for the foreseeable future. Not that it would change anything between them. Theirs was still only a temporary arrangement, until his father was well again.

He'd swing by the job site today and see how things stood. Then he'd work on finding them a place to live until her house was available. After this morning, he knew he couldn't continue sharing a room with Trisha and stick to the terms of their arrangement. His hands clenched, yet he still felt the soft warmth of her skin. He smelled the antiseptic air of the hospital, but remembered her sweet flowery scent. They needed a place like they'd had in Kuwait—two bedrooms, two baths. That way he'd only see her when they ate. That way he would not sleep with her and fight to keep his hands off her. Not have to watch her as she dressed and clamp down on his desire to prevent himself from launching across the room and tumbling her into the bed. Not have to see that honey-sweet skin that drew him like a magnet, not have to remember the tantalizing glimpse of rosy-tipped nipples, long silky legs, shiny satiny hair...

Celibacy was a killer. It had been over two years since he'd slept with a woman. That must be why he was reacting this way. Once they were established in their own place, with separate bedrooms and their old routine, he'd be fine. He'd managed this past year without touching her, without watching every move she made, without craving her. He could resume as soon as they found a place of their own.

He pushed away and started back to the waiting room. In the doorway he paused, his eyes drawn instantly to Trisha. She was laughing at something Becky had said. For a moment a deep longing pushed up from the very heart of him. She'd often smiled at him over the past decade. But it had always been a polite smile, never loving and open like the ones she shared with Becky. Her entire face was lit with amusement, and love for his sister. Her dark eyes sparkled and shimmered in humor and her straight white teeth shone evenly behind her delicate lips.

Cole stepped into the room, wanting that warmth and shared humor directed at him. But when she saw him, her face froze, then the polite mask he knew so well dropped into place.

"Ready to leave?" Trisha asked as she rose.

"Yes. I want to run by the construction site. We'll come back tonight. Dad's waiting for you, Becky. Mom went to the business office to finalize a few things. She'll be back in a little while. I think he'll sleep the rest of the day. The doctor's going to be here tonight so we'll get our answers then.''

Becky bade them both a cheery goodbye and went to take her turn visiting her dad.

In only moments Cole and Trisha were in the car.

''I'll drop you off at the house before I head for the construction site.''

''So your dad asked you to take over,'' she confirmed.

''Yes, just as you predicted. It changes nothing between us, though. Remember that.''

She clenched her teeth. ''Do you really think I'm such a mercenary? That now that you'll have a company to run I'll expect lavish amounts of money to spend? That I expect you to set me up in some sort of fancy style when we divorce? I told you I don't need any money.''

He shrugged. ''Just making sure you know the rules didn't change.''

''Stop comparing me to Diane, Cole. I'm not like her. I don't have a gambling problem. I'm not lying to you about any debts I've run up, and I certainly don't have a lover on the side.''

''Yet,'' he ground out.

''What does that mean?'' She glared at him.

''What about your declaration this morning about finding another man?''

She tilted her head and watched him, trying to figure out exactly why he seemed angry.

You don't need another man, I'm man enough for you. You're mine and I'm not letting you go.

She watched for endless minutes, but his lips remained firmly together, thinned with anger barely held in check. Okay, so he wasn't going to say that, but she wouldn't let him get away with what he had said.

''You know I meant after the divorce. When I'm single I'd like to attract someone. Do you want me to remain alone the rest of my life?''

He was silent, hearing her words echo in his mind. Alone the rest of her life? No, he couldn't ask that. Couldn't expect that. She was young, only twenty-seven. She had her whole life before her. Just because she helped him out when he needed it this past year was no reason to expect her to devote herself to his memory once they were divorced.

Alone the rest of her life.

Hell, he was going to be alone the rest of his. What was the big deal? At least that way there'd be no one to steal his money, no one to trash his heart. He'd be in control of every aspect. He would be content to work, visit with friends. Marriage wasn't for him.

She liked being part of a couple.

If he was honest, he'd admit he had enjoyed the past year with her.

"I know you got a raw deal with Diane, but I'm not her and I don't want to keep getting her backwash. I'll stay with you until your dad is better, then I'm finding a man who will want to build a future together. After seeing pictures of Tyler and Trevor and hearing Becky talk, I want children more than ever. I want at least three. I'm all alone in the world, Cole. I need a family to love."

He pulled into the driveway.

"Just drop me off. I'll fix something for dinner. Can you be home by six?" She had thrust open the door when he pulled up by the house, and now she slammed it behind her.

Waiting only for his nod, Trisha hurried toward the steps, not wanting to even think. She had to find a way to get this man to change his mind about her or find it in herself to get over him and get on with her life.

Becky brought Peggy Langford home after a second visit with her husband. Not able to stay, Becky again invited Trisha and Cole to dinner later in the week and then kissed her mother goodbye.

"They're planning to operate tomorrow," Peggy said sadly as she trailed into the kitchen.

"Let me fix you a cup of tea," Trisha said. "Sit down and rest, you need to keep your strength up for Matt." She bustled about the familiar kitchen fixing her mother-in-law a hot cup of tea, chatting with her as she tried to take her mind off the seriousness of her husband's illness.

"I'm so glad you and Cole could come home, Trisha. Becky is so busy with the boys and Tom and with being pregnant, I don't want her worrying too much. But I've needed someone. You know I've always depended on Matt so much. Maybe too much. I don't know what I'll do if he doesn't recover."

"He'll be fine, you have to hold on to that. He's getting the best care possible and has one of the finest doctors in Virginia. You were such a help to me when Daddy was so sick, I'm glad I can be here for you."

Peggy nodded, taking a sip of tea, her eyes flooding with tears. "I was sorry your father died when he did. It gave us all a jolt of realization of our own mortality. Maybe that was what Cole needed to propose to you. At least that's one less thing I have to worry about—Cole's happiness."

Trisha smiled, hoping the expression on her face looked happy. Her heart ached for the woman and her pain. At least for the time being she and Cole could keep the knowledge from his parents that they wouldn't be living happily ever after. He'd been right to ask her to stay with him until his father recovered. She'd do her part to the bitter end.

Settling Peggy down to rest, Trisha wandered around the house, finally moving to the big swing that hung from one of the old oak trees in the backyard. It reminded her of the swing at her own home. She had yet to notify the realty company that it was time to give notice to her tenants.

She had brought her notepad to check off some of the items on her list and began to make a new one. First, new clothes, something with a little more oomph than what she normally wore. If the fancy underwear didn't work to catch Cole's attention, maybe she'd try something a little more blatant. Then there was her hair. Should she get it cut? She'd ask Becky. How about makeup? And provocative moves? Those she needed to practice. She wasn't used to flirting openly with anyone. Was that a learned trait? She sure hoped so. Drifting back and forth on the swing in the dappled shade, she gazed off into space. Maybe she should run by the library. She could visit with her old colleagues and check out any books on flirting.

She remembered the old checking account she'd shared with her father. She needed to check its balance, check the signature card. She jotted a note. If she could do more of the cooking, she could fix Cole's favorite meals. She had carefully listened to him when he complimented her on the meals in Kuwait and knew what he liked best. Drat, she needed to check if there were any other investments her dad had had.

The list was becoming a mishmash of different topics. She leaned back in the swing and let her imagination soar, imagining herself with Cole. First chance she got, she was buying new clothes!

Late that afternoon, Cole pulled into the driveway bone tired. He had reviewed the standings at the two sites in progress, visited Langford Construction's small central office downtown and quickly scanned the financial statements. The business was in trouble. His father had not been working up to standard for months. There were labor problems, material shortages and bills in arrears. One site was in danger of losing its financial backing. Just what he needed—a troubled company to deal with, in addition to everything else. Why had his dad let things slide? Had his health been so bad for so long? Why hadn't he said something earlier?

Sighing softly, he climbed out of the car and headed into the kitchen. Opening the door, Cole paused a moment as he watched Trisha and his mother working together preparing the evening meal. They'd all go back to the hospital in another hour or so and again tomorrow for the surgery. Damn, he was tired. And depressed.

"Cole!" Trisha spun around when she heard the slight click of the screen door and smiled in warm welcome. Taking three small steps, she flung herself against his chest and reached up with her arms to pull his head down.

Instinctively Cole wrapped his arms around her and returned the kiss. He felt warmth and softness, smelled sweetness and innocence, tasted hunger and desire. The mouth-watering aromas of ham and sweet potatoes baking in the oven mingled with the light flowery fragrance that was Trisha's own. Her mouth welcomed his in a kiss so distracting that for a split second he forgot where he was. He could only feel the armful of soft femininity that enveloped him.

Pulling back slightly, Trisha looked at him with warning. "How was your day?" Slowly she released him, even more slowly pushed away as his arms reluctantly opened.

"Hectic. Trouble at both sites, a ton of paperwork waiting at the office." What was she doing? Except for their kiss at the wedding, he'd never kissed her. And that chaste kiss had very little in common with the one she'd just given him.

His mother hurried over, her face wrinkled in worry. "Oh no, not your father's company. Cole, you'll have to do something."

"Of course I will, Mom." He brushed a kiss against her cheek. "The cavalry arrived just in time. You don't need to worry, I can turn things around in a few weeks. Dinner smells wonderful. How long before we eat?"

"Another twenty minutes. If you want to take a quick shower, there's time," Trisha said as she turned back to the biscuit dough she'd been rolling, remembering his routine from Kuwait. Her insides felt squishy from his kiss. She knew he was stunned at her flinging herself against him, but she planned to do all she could to maintain their farce before his mother. She couldn't let Peggy suspect everything wasn't perfect in her son's marriage. Trisha would have to explain to Cole, though, lest he think she'd lost her mind.

"A shower would be just what I need." He ran his fingers through his hair as he started for the hall bathroom. What game was she playing? He didn't think they'd touched more than a dozen times in all the years he'd known her. But that kiss hadn't been some platonic peck. It had been one openmouthed, hot-honey, soul-searing kiss.

Stripping off his clothes, he ran the water hot and stepped beneath the spray. For a second he could feel the impression of Trisha's body against his, her arms pulling him closer, the soft press of her breasts against his chest. In the steamy bathroom he could still smell the sweet scent of her. Every time he brushed past her, he'd smell the soft scent that was Trisha's own. Blindfolded, he could find her by her own special fragrance.

The feel of her in his arms aroused him. It had been too long since he'd made love. That was all. Reaching out, he shut off the hot water and stood beneath the cold spray. He had too much to worry about with his father's surgery, his mother's concerns and now the problems at the construction sites. He didn't need a complication in the form of some unmanageable attraction for Trisha. Something had to be done, and fast, to regain the distance they'd maintained in Kuwait.

Cole dressed in clean jeans and a soft cotton shirt. When he joined his mother and Trisha in the kitchen, they were setting the table. He helped—anything to keep his eyes from Trisha.

But when they sat to eat, his mother placed him opposite his wife. Cole studied her as she talked easily with his mother, keeping the conversation firmly upbeat and on happy topics. They discussed the rose show and the prize his

mother had won. Trisha asked after all the neighbors and if
his mother had heard anything about her tenants. Her voice
was soft and compelling, a husky alto that sent tendrils of
awareness through him. Cole liked the tenor, liked the ca-
dence. He'd known her for years, yet never appreciated how
sexy her voice sounded. What would it be like in the dark,
whispering words of love?

Scowling at his wayward thoughts, he tried to focus on the
conversation. Realizing both women were staring at him, he
blinked.

"What?"

"I asked what was wrong at the company," his mother
said gently.

"Just needs Dad's hand. I'll step in until he's better,"
Cole said.

"If he gets better." His mother's eyes filled with tears.

"He will," Cole stated firmly.

"Even if he does, the company's grown too large for one
man to run," Peggy said.

"Nonsense, Dad's done it for years."

"But he's not as young as he used to be."

"He'll be fine, Mom."

"And he'll recover so much faster knowing Cole is in
charge while he's gone," Trisha added, reaching out to grasp
the older woman's hand in comfort. "That's one less worry
Matt will have. He can concentrate on getting well."

"Maybe Matt should retire," Peggy said hesitantly.

Trisha nodded. "If he wants. He could consider the option. I'm sure Cole would take over the business. Wouldn't
you?" She turned her dark eyes on him. "Wouldn't you,
Cole?"

He stared at her, trying to discern what convoluted
thoughts spun in her mind. Why was she pushing him so
hard to take over his father's business? Did she plan to hang
on and make the most of the turn of events? Langford
Construction had been a big company before he left for

Kuwait. It could easily turn around, if it had some aggressive management. He could do it, and she knew it.

"I'll run it as long as Dad needs me," he said slowly, wanting once again to make sure Trisha knew he had not changed his plans. They had an agreement. He would enforce it. He would make sure she knew there was not going to be a repeat of history. This time his wife would not take all his money and move on to greener pastures.

He'd told her. As late as this morning. So just what was her game?

Trisha smiled slowly as she watched Cole's suspicious gaze. She knew what he was thinking, trying to figure out how she planned to hurt him the way Diane had. Well, he was in for a surprise. She had no intention of hurting him. She loved him. She only wanted to be able to prove that to him, and make him aware of her.

Cole needed the responsibility of Langford Construction. His dad would give him an important spot in the company if he showed any interest in it. And that vote of confidence would go a long way to making life easier for the tough, bitter man who thought his world had ended a couple of years ago. She knew from Becky's letters that his father wanted out. Matt wanted to take time to enjoy life with his wife, maybe do some traveling, turn over the day-to-day operations to his son.

Cole had to stop being so suspicious of everyone and everything. It was time he took the blessings life offered him and made the most of them.

"We should be getting to the hospital soon," Peggy said, unaware of the rising tension between the others.

"Maybe Trisha should stay home," Cole said, frowning at her.

"Why?" Startled, she stared at him. She had planned to go tonight with everyone else. Was he already trying to wean her away from his life?

"The stress is too much for you, darling. I need you strong for me. To help me make it through this hard time."

"You look tired. I know the flight home was a killer, and we're not going to be there that long. Dad can see you after the operation. We're just going to meet with the doctor, pop in to see Dad, then come home."

Unexpectedly Trisha felt cherished. It had been a long time since anyone had thought about her, had taken care of her. It wouldn't be hard to stay home. She was tired and dreaded going back to the hospital. It brought back such sad memories of when her own father had been so ill. But she would have gone had Cole asked her.

"I could clean up here and get to bed early," she said slowly.

"Cole's right. I should have thought of it. Get a good night's rest. Tomorrow will be so stressful, until we know the results of the surgery," Peggy said, concern in her every gesture.

"Trisha doesn't have to go tomorrow, either." He knew how hard it was for her to be at the hospital. There was no reason for her to endure painful memories during his father's operation. According to the surgeon's earlier comments, the operation would take hours. Then Matt would spend time in the recovery room before anyone could see him. Cole was not going to make Trisha go through all that. She didn't need that kind of strain.

"Oh, but—" his mother started to protest.

"Yes, I'll go tomorrow," Trisha said.

"Are you sure?" he asked softly, wanting to shelter her from the situation if he could. He didn't want her hurt. Theirs might be a temporary marriage, but he felt the age-old need to protect his wife.

She nodded. "I want to be there." She would hate it. She would live in fear until they knew the outcome. She hoped so desperately that Cole's father recovered, that he wouldn't lose his father as she had hers. It would be hard, but she wanted to do it. She needed to show her husband she could be counted on in every way.

"It will be a long day," he warned.

Trisha nodded. She remembered the nightmare of her father's illness. So many hours when she sat beside his bed, willing him to live, praying for his recovery. The endless minutes when he never knew she was there. In the end it hadn't mattered. He'd died peacefully in his sleep in the wee hours.

"I'll take some knitting, something to help pass the time." Peggy was resolute, knowing her husband's life was threatened.

"We'll be there first thing in the morning. Becky and Tom are coming, too, aren't they?" Cole asked.

His mother nodded, smiling sadly. Everyone knew the fear she faced. Trisha blinked back tears and tried not to imagine herself in a similar situation. What if it were Cole whose life hung in the balance? What if she didn't know for sure whether he'd be there with her tomorrow night? The anguish pierced her. She couldn't stand it. Even if she was unable to change his mind about marriage, she had the consolation of knowing he'd be alive and well somewhere in the world. She glanced at him, meeting his fierce stare, hoping her expression gave nothing away.

"We'll be back before nine. Go to bed, honey, you look tired," he said gruffly, standing and pulling out the chair for his mother. He didn't like tears in Trisha's eyes. It reminded him of the night he'd found her on her back porch. He hadn't liked it then, and he hated it now. He wanted to see her smile, laugh, like she had with Becky this afternoon. He wanted her to smile at him like that, just once.

Cole came awake the next morning with an armful of sweet, warm femininity. Trisha lay sprawled all over him, one satiny thigh between his, her breasts snuggling against his rib cage, her silky hair spread across his chest and shoulder like a blanket, one warm arm encircling him. Both of his arms surrounded her. She was fast asleep.

Instantly Cole became totally awake, aware, aroused. Lying still, he felt the soft brush of her moist breath caress his nipple as she breathed deeply, in and out. He felt the steady slow beat of her heart against his ribs, touched the velvet texture of her skin as one hand skimmed gently over her bottom. His T-shirt offered scant covering for her tantalizing body. What the sweet hell was she doing sprawled all over him while sleeping? The queen-size bed should be plenty big enough for the two of them to sleep without touching.

He had to find them a place to stay. He couldn't take much more of this without doing something he'd regret.

Perspiration broke out on his forehead as he sought to control the sudden reaction to her closeness. His own heart rate sped up. He felt a strong urgent ache low in his belly. God, she was tempting. Her curves cried out for his caress. Her hair begged him to tangle his fingertips in it and feel the silky thickness, the gentle ripple of waves. Her lips tantalized him, tempting him to cover them with his own and lose himself in her soft feminine beauty.

Struggling with temptation as old and strong as time, he did nothing. He remained perfectly still, yet absorbed every aspect of their compromising situation. When she awoke she'd probably start screaming. *This* had definitely not been part of their bargain. He had promised a platonic relationship, nothing more.

Why had his mother bought this blasted bed? In the bunk beds he'd had since childhood, they'd never have ended up like this. It would have been easy to maintain their platonic relationship. Now he didn't know if he could open his arms and release her.

He should move away. She was asleep; she'd never know. He should slip out from beneath her, climb out of bed and head for the shower. Another cold one. That's what he should do.

What he would do in just another minute.

But for one more minute he'd savor the delectable sensations of holding Trisha in his arms. Treasure the passion that rioted through him as he became minutely aware of the hard bead of her nipples, of the sensuous heat of her thigh nestled up against his sex, of her sweet scent enveloping him in a haze of sexual awareness.

He wanted her. He wanted to kiss her deeply, taste the honey sweetness that he'd tasted last night when he'd come home from work. He wanted to fondle her, caress her silky skin, touch every inch of her, learn all her secrets. But mostly he wanted to plunge into the feminine heat that waited for a lover's touch. Trembling slightly with the effort it cost him to remain still, he let his imagination take flight, soaring with the thrill of making love with Trisha. He hadn't been totally oblivious to her over the past year. It had surprised him once or twice, a fleeting, compelling thought of making love with his wife. But he'd remembered Diane, and the risk of another debacle had been too great. He didn't want to get tangled up in any kind of relationship that would leave him as vulnerable as the last one had.

The rapid heartbeat beneath her right ear thrummed. Blinking slowly, Trisha stretched like a boneless cat. Suddenly she became aware of exactly where she was lying, pressed up against a most decidedly male body. Stunned, she raised her head and met Cole's amused gaze.

"Awake?" he asked, his arms still holding her.

Awake and extremely aware of her proximity to Cole. Her brown eyes widened in shock and for a moment she couldn't move. "What are you doing on my side?" she said, stacking her hands on his chest and gazing at him after glancing around the bed. Her skin tingled where he touched her. Slowly she met his gaze, holding it, wondering what he saw as he looked at her.

"Your side? Since when did we divvy up the bed?" He liked the way she appeared flustered, confused, yet kept striving for control. Usually more reserved, the change charmed him.

"Well, this is the side I climbed into last night. Alone, I might add. And I notice you're very much on it now," she defended, meeting his gaze bravely.

He gave a lazy grin. "Maybe I want this side."

"Well, you should have said something last night." She shifted slightly, moving to get to the far side. She grew instantly aware of her bare leg tangled with his, her T-shirt riding up by her waist. His hand was on her bare bottom! He felt like a furnace beneath her.

"Cole!" Heat suffused. Her skin felt as if it were on fire.

"Be reasonable, Trisha. Here I was, calmly sleeping on my back and you climbed all over me. You can't blame me." He moved his hand a scant centimeter, unwilling to relinquish his hold. The sexy feel of her skin was a temptation he wasn't strong enough to refuse. He was as hard as a man got and knew there would be nothing to assuage the pulsing desire that pounded through him. She'd be scared out of her mind if he rolled her over and began to make love to her. For a few moments longer he'd endure the agony.

It was as intimate a position as she'd ever experienced. Trisha felt every inch of his skin as it inflamed her own. His hand was the least of it. His hot body lay beneath hers, her leg felt the crinkly hair of his muscular thighs. She could feel—

She dropped her head against his shoulder, unable to face him at the moment. For a long second there was silence. She wanted to die. Wanted to melt away so she never had to endure the embarrassment that facing him would produce.

"Why don't you slip off that silly T-shirt and kiss me, let me make love to you? We've both wanted this for so long, Trisha."

She longed for the words. Just once, couldn't he read her mind?

"Trisha, I think we need to talk about this," Cole said reasonably.

She slipped over to the side and scrambled to her feet beside the bed. "Talk about what?" She backed away from temptation, yanking down the T-shirt while she tried to bring some rational thought process to bear. He was probably as embarrassed as she, and he was right, he'd done nothing. She'd been the one on top of him.

"Talk about this and why you kissed me last night." Cole sat up in bed, fluffed up a couple of pillows and leaned back against the headboard. The sheet fell to his waist, his muscular legs clearly defined beneath the soft cotton.

Trisha resolutely kept her eyes on his. "I only kissed you to reassure your mother that our marriage was normal. She mentioned how relieved she was not to have to worry about your happiness anymore. Wasn't that your reason for continuing this charade of a marriage now that we're back in the States? To reassure your folks until your father is well?"

Where was a robe when she needed it? They had packed too hastily in Kuwait. She needed more clothes.

"Yes, that was the reason. I just wondered if that was your reason as well, that's all. Especially in light of waking up with you all over me." The humor appealed to him. He chuckled softly.

"Dammit, Cole, it's not funny. You stay on your side of the bed." *Or I'll lose what little control I have around you.* How had she ever thought she could seduce the man? He hadn't noticed her as a woman in all the years he'd known her. Why did she think she had a chance in the few weeks until his father recovered? She had practically been naked in his arms and he was laughing.

And she'd panicked.

He snapped back the sheets in a sudden move and stalked over to her. Trisha stared at him. He was overwhelmingly masculine! She couldn't keep her eyes from tracking down his chest to his white briefs, down his long muscular legs, back up to his wide tanned chest, skimming across the obvious bulge behind the briefs. Fire scorched her cheeks and she jerked her gaze up to meet his. Humor had fled. Something else, dark and steady, replaced it.

In two steps he crowded against her, drawing her into his arms, his mouth descending until he crushed hers beneath his. The shock of the move held Trisha immobile. Then feelings like she'd never known overtook her being. Heat curled deep in her belly as shimmering waves of desire flooded her limbs, rendering her legs weak, her hands incapable of pushing him away, as the small part of sanity that remained urged her to do.

When his lips moved against hers, Trisha responded. Helpless against the onslaught, she ignored the warning signals emitted from her brain and gave way to the passion enveloping her. For long moments she reveled in the exquisite sensations shimmering through her. Time was forgotten. The bedroom became a cloud, the sunshine in the window exploded into rainbows of pleasure as she floated on pure delight.

Four

Breathing hard, Cole pulled back, his eyes narrowed as he gazed down at her flushed face.

"If it's sex games you want to play, Trish, just let me know. I've been without a woman for over two years. It wouldn't take much to trigger me. If that's what you want for a few weeks, I'm more than willing."

The hard press against her belly proved his point, just as his fingers tangled hard in her hair demonstrated the iron control he held on his emotions.

"Cole?" Peggy Langford knocked on the door. "Cole, are you awake? You have a long-distance call from Markham International."

"Be right there, Mom," he called in response. His eyes glittered down into Trisha's, his hands slowly unwinding from her hair. "Mark my place, sweetheart, and we'll continue this discussion after I take the call," he said as he turned swiftly and drew on his jeans, zipping them as he headed out the door.

Trisha stood absolutely still, stunned. Her heart rate frantic, she took a deep breath. His words echoed around and around in her mind. *Sex games...without a woman for over two years.* God, she had been hoping to seduce him with some indication of affection. Was he talking about a few nights of mindless sex? She didn't want a relationship like that. Not exactly. Would it lead to something else perhaps?

Grabbing her clothes, she headed for the bathroom. Carefully locking the door behind her, she turned on the shower, stripped off his T-shirt and stepped beneath the soothing spray. What had happened? She wanted what he offered, but not like that. Sighing with disappointment, she began to suspect her goal was hopeless. She wanted at least some affection, a certain level of caring from him. She knew he didn't love her, might never trust another woman again after the mess of his first marriage. But she had hoped for the closeness of friendship at least.

Instead she felt as if he'd made an offer to her just as he would have to any available woman. No longer did she feel cherished as she had last night when he suggested she stay home. She wasn't sure if she should feel insulted or flattered that he offered sex games. At least he wasn't repulsed by her.

And wasn't that what she wanted? For him to see her as an available, desirable woman? One who would relish being in his arms, delight in learning the secrets of his body, in sharing hers. One who would enjoy nights with him beyond anything she'd known.

Yet without affection, without love, was there any possibility of a future? Could she make love with him and then walk away unscathed in a few weeks?

Cole dragged his fingers through his hair as he hurried down the stairs to the kitchen. Giving his mother a quick kiss on the cheek in passing, he snatched up the phone, but his thoughts remained with Trisha.

He'd pushed too hard. What had come over him? She'd seemed embarrassed, almost scared when she flounced off the bed. He'd been piqued enough to want to push a little, offering what he knew would probably scare her to death. Yet the need deep in him slammed strong. And from the way she reacted to his kisses, she wasn't totally averse to the notion. Who would have expected his shy, somewhat prim little wife to kiss so explosively? It made him wonder again what she'd be like in bed. Obviously she wouldn't be the same quiet woman he had spent the past year with. If her kisses were an indication, she'd be a fireball—honey-hot and sweet. He was getting hard just thinking about it.

"Langford here," he said into the receiver. Listening for a moment, he frowned. "No way to expedite?" Just what he needed, another problem. What would Trisha do? The fact that their belongings were being held up and probably wouldn't arrive for another six weeks would concern her, as well.

He hung up impatiently, turned to head back to the bedroom. Couldn't one thing work out smoothly?

"We need to leave soon," his mother said gently from across the kitchen. She looked older today, frightened.

"We'll be down in plenty of time, Mom," Cole said gently, going across to give her a hug, noting almost impassively how different she felt in his arms than Trisha. He gave her a quick kiss, anxious to get back upstairs. Once he reached the top of the stairs, he heard the shower. She hadn't waited. The disappointment that hit showed he had really hoped she would.

"Trisha, you going to hog the bathroom all morning?" Cole banged on the closed door, impatient to see her again. She'd been behind that door for over a half hour. He'd come back to their room ready to resume where they'd left off, and found her ensconced in the bath. Aggravated, he paced the narrow space between the bed and the wall. Finally giving in to his impatience, he'd moved to the hall, knocking on the door.

"I'm almost ready," she called. Gazing at her reflection in the mirror, Trisha took a deep breath, tried to quiet the roiling nerves that gave her no rest. She had to face him again. There was no way she could spend the rest of her life in the bathroom. But what would she say? Do? And what if he kissed her again? She'd be helpless to resist, that much she did know. And why should she? They were married. Maybe it would show him they belonged together.

Yeah, right.

Taking a deep breath, she turned and opened the door. And almost walked right into the solid wall of his chest.

"Oh." Startled, she glanced up.

Cole stared down at her with hungry eyes. Slowly he reached out and wrapped a tendril of hair around one finger, anchoring her in place as surely as if he'd poured cement around her. She dropped her eyes to his broad chest and her longings rose. Daringly she let one hand drift up and permitted her fingertips to brush against the muscles that stretched beneath his tanned skin.

She heard him suck in his breath sharply and immediately met his heated gaze. The reckless abandonment of old habits surprised her. Slowly she took a deep breath and smiled.

"Mom's worried we won't get to the hospital in time," he said, his thumb rubbing over the silky strand of hair twirled around his fingers.

"I didn't mean to be so long in the bathroom," she said, her voice husky with emotion. "Was the call important?" *Important enough to interrupt us?*

"You could say that. There's been a snafu with shipping our personal things. They won't be here for another six weeks."

"Six weeks!" Gone were the amorous feelings coursing through her as the impact of what he told her hit hard. "Cole, I'm right in the midst of revisions. I need my computer. I can't wait another week, much less six."

"We'll rent you one. You kept your chapters on floppies, didn't you? Brought them home with you?"

"Yes." The momentary panic eased.

"In fact, I think I saw an extra computer at the Windmere site that you could use," he said, slowly tugging her closer. He liked the feel of her hand on his chest, liked the softness of her hair tangled in his fingers. He wanted to explore her sweetness once more. Why had he never thought seriously about Trisha in his bed before today? If she were willing to change the terms of their agreement for the remaining time they were together, he'd be a fool to turn down what he wanted just because he'd made a rash promise a year ago. He was her husband. Everyone in the world thought they were sleeping together. Who would it hurt if they did?

"Wouldn't I be in your way?" She knew things were happening too fast, but keeping a tight rein on her control proved harder than anything. She'd longed for some physical contact with him for so long she couldn't resist when he offered, no matter what the reasons. Stepping closer, she skimmed her hand up his chest to his shoulder, around the nape of his neck, brushing against the thick hair that grew a little long. Daringly Trisha stepped closer, letting her breasts lightly brush against him.

His fingers threaded into her hair and he drew her even closer, lowering his mouth to gently touch the parted lips that awaited. The explosive reaction to that light touch startled him. He was again surprised to find the feelings so intense. Giving in to the invitation, he gently plunged into her mouth with his tongue, meeting hers, discovering all the delights of her moist warmth.

"You pack a wallop, lady," he said, drawing back as he heard his mother moving downstairs. They were out in the open in the hallway. He had to get dressed, get his mother to the hospital before eight, and all he could think of was taking Trisha back to their bed, stripping her down and making slow, hot love to her all day.

"You're not so bad yourself," she said, smiling shyly. Reluctantly bringing her hand down, she stepped around him and headed toward their room. "The bathroom's all yours."

Sex games, sex games, sex games, echoed around and around in Trisha's mind as Cole swiftly drove to the hospital. She had insisted on sitting in the back, letting Peggy sit in front beside her son. Trisha had hoped the distance would give her some calming perspective, but she couldn't find any watching his every move. She loved the way he looked, his sun-bleached hair that definitely needed a trim soon, his angular jaw so confidently set as he faced the day's challenges. Loved his understated strength that radiated in all situations. It wasn't only physical strength from working in construction, but the strength of determination and purpose that sat so well in him. Even the blow of losing so much because of Diane hadn't slowed him down.

Trisha began to consider whether she ought to regroup, to hold off on her nebulous plan of attack and see exactly what Cole offered. She started to believe she should take what she could get from him, and let the dreams of love and affection simmer. Maybe he'd grow to love her. Maybe he'd enjoy a sexual relationship enough that he'd want to stay married. Would that be enough for her? Would marriage without Cole's love be preferable to life alone?

They found Becky and Tom already waiting at the hospital. So began an endless day. There was nothing to do but wait while the surgeon used his skill to save the life of Matt Langford. Peggy had brought knitting. Becky and Trisha talked, walked on the lawn, returned to eat a scant lunch at the hospital cafeteria.

Finally, just after two, the surgeon came to tell them the operation had been a success.

"He's in recovery now. You can peek in on him, one at a time. But he won't know you're there. In fact, it will be tomorrow morning before he is fully awake and aware again. I suggest you see him now and then return later, or even wait until tomorrow. He's going to be fine."

Peggy had tears running down her cheeks. Becky turned to Tom and he enfolded her in his arms. Trisha blinked back tears of relief, startled when Cole put his arm around her shoulders and hugged her gently.

"You doing okay?" he whispered.

She nodded. "I'm so glad he's going to be okay. How are you doing?"

"I'm feeling a whole lot better than I have since we got the call."

Peggy wanted to stay to see her husband, stay in the room with him even if he didn't know she was there. Cole, confident his father was on the road to recovery, was anxious to get to the construction sites and get busy working to save the company. He invited Trisha to go with him, to check out the extra computer. Making sure Peggy was set, they left.

Windmere was hot and dusty. The earth had been graded and smoothed in preparation for the houses that were already laid out. Several lonely trees clung to the dusty ground, evidence of Matt Langford's effort to retain the old growth where possible. Two dozen houses stood in various stages of construction, framing up in some, plumbing already begun in others. None had the walls as yet and Trisha was intrigued to look through the wood frames at the expanses that would one day be rooms.

Men were everywhere, hammering nails, sawing wood, stringing wire. The activity looked chaotic yet Trisha knew each man was an expert at his job and the buildings were going up efficiently.

Cole unlocked the construction trailer and threw open the door. Peering inside curiously, Trisha paused for a moment while he flicked on the air conditioner. The trailer was stifling; they'd need the cooling system operating on high to keep it manageable in the hot Virginia summer.

There were two desks, an assortment of filing cabinets and a drafting table with blueprints and schematics scattered across it. The desks were piled high with stacks of papers, permits and invoices, notes of modifications and sales literature.

"You can use that desk today, that computer. Just dump the stuff from the desk onto mine. I have to go through everything to get a handle on what's going on," Cole said casually, turning to flip on the answering machine.

As the messages unwound, Trisha walked over to the desk indicated and began to gather up the stacks of papers. She placed them on the edge of Cole's desk, noticing how close the desks were. She would not have the luxury of being on her own in a quiet room to create; she'd be in the middle of a working construction site, with the boss man right beside her. A very disturbing boss man, at that.

She sat before the computer, pleased to discover it was the same model as the one she had. Now, she thought as she pressed the on button, if it only had the same word processor she'd be back in business. When the main menu came up, she was pleased to see it did. Booting up the program, she withdrew her floppies from her bag, conscious every second of Cole sitting only a half-dozen feet away, his eyes watching her every move.

She flashed a frown. "Don't you have work to do?"

He paused the answering machine and grinned at her in a definitely superior male fashion. "I'm doing it. I can listen to the messages while I watch you. A man likes a pretty view."

She turned back to the computer, the unexpected compliment flooding her with pleasure. She wasn't sure what his game was just now—probably a prelude to getting her back where they'd left off that morning—but it was pleasing to have the compliment. It was even better than one she would have thought up for him to say and meant more since it came spontaneously.

Trisha pulled up the first chapter of her latest book and immediately tried to catch up the story line. Her editor liked the manuscript, liked the continuing main character and was impatient for the revisions on this one to be delivered. She was ahead of schedule. If she completed it early, her publisher had promised they would bump her up in the release schedule.

Men came and went, discussing needs and plans with Cole. She watched him talk to them, go over blueprints and schematics. Pretending to work, she noticed how he kept his impatience under control, how quickly he found problems and offered solutions.

Then he left the trailer to show the men what he wanted, shrugging out of his shirt, wearing only the T-shirt that matched the one she used as a nightie.

Trisha gave up all pretense of writing and went to the window. Cole picked up a tool belt and strapped it on. She smiled. It reminded her of an old-fashioned gunslinger. The belt hung on his slim hips, riding low. The jeans were snug, displaying the long length of his muscular legs. He plopped on the hard hat and turned unexpectedly, his gaze connecting with hers through the dusty glass. Trisha stared back, fascinated. Caught up in the heat of his eyes, she couldn't move if she tried. Then he smiled slowly, oh so smugly, and turned back to the construction worker at his side.

"Think you're so smart to catch me out, don't you?" she murmured. "But I caught you out, too, Mr. Know-it-all."

It was only when she saw Cole heading back toward the trailer that she dashed over to the computer and began to read what was on the monitor.

She focused on her plot, the clues she hoped were not too obvious, the characterization, delving more and more into the reasons and motives of the protagonists, trying to build suspense as the hero faced danger again and again.

When had her hero begun to resemble Cole? When had the female in this book begun to resemble herself? She flicked a quick glance up as Cole strode into the trailer.

"Miss me?" he asked arrogantly.

"Oh, were you gone?"

Chuckling, he tossed aside the belt and hat and confidently crossed the trailer and leaned over her, resting his hands on the arms of her chair.

"As if I didn't see you in the window."

"Why were you looking?"

"Just to see what I saw." He stared down at her without moving.

Trisha became nervous, uncomfortable with the lengthening silence, with the silent exchange waging between them. She rested her hands on his hot arms, clutching for sanity's sake.

"This isn't a good idea," she said breathlessly, wishing with all her heart he'd kiss her.

"What isn't?" His voice was like hot wine, intoxicating every nerve ending as his eyes never left hers.

"Sex ga— I mean trying to work here." God, she hadn't said it, had she? Just because she had thought of nothing else since he said it, please don't let her have said it out loud.

His breath brushed across her cheeks. Suddenly her lips tingled. She wished he'd kiss her like he had that morning, hot and hard and passionately. She liked the way she felt when he kissed her, the way her body tingled and responded. Was it like an addiction? The more she had, the more she'd crave?

She slid her hands up his arms, across his shoulders and to his neck, tugging experimentally. Cole gave a half smile and lowered his head to her urging.

Her mouth was waiting when he closed the distance and kissed her. He could feel her fingers thread through his hair, pulling him closer and closer. Drawing her to her feet, he wrapped his arms around her and molded her body to his.

"Say, Cole— Oops, bad timing." The door slammed shut.

Trisha pulled back, horrified. "It was one of the men," she exclaimed.

"Sounded like it." Cole turned and headed out the door.

Trisha sank back down on her chair. There was no way she was going to get any work done here. They had just proved that. And she didn't want Cole's authority undermined by any hanky-panky on-site with his wife. She had to see if she could take the computer home and work there.

Besides, she had accomplished very little today. She needed privacy to be able to concentrate on her book. It was too easy to look up and let her gaze feast on the sexy image her husband projected.

Cole didn't return for almost a half hour. When he did, Trisha was ready to leave.

"I called the hospital. Your mom's gone home. Your dad's doing as expected, still asleep. I'm ready to go home when you are. Can I take the computer? Working here isn't an option." She used her best librarian voice. She refused to meet his eyes, but focused on his chin. She didn't want to get distracted before they got home.

"Yes to going home, yes to taking the computer." He wasn't sorry she wouldn't be working at the trailer. He'd hardly been able to concentrate on the work at the site; he'd been thinking about her. Especially this past half hour.

"Tell me about the book you're working on," Cole invited as he drove away from the building site. It occurred to him he had never really asked about her work. He'd been too distracted and furious at the beginning of their marriage. Then they had fallen into a pattern of working and eating and sleeping that had excluded much interchange between them. Gradually his anger toward Diane had faded; the anger at himself for being so oblivious had gone. But he'd never thought to ask Trisha about her work. She wrote every day and he didn't know if she still liked writing or found it tedious. If she were worried about writer's block or if the words poured from her.

"It's another John Taylor book. He's the ex-CIA agent that solved the other mysteries," she said, wondering why Cole asked. He'd never seemed interested in her work.

"You have the same hero in every book?"

She nodded. "Yes. I like him."

"Does he remind you of me? Did you pattern your hero after me? Are there any romantic elements in the book that I should look at?"

"Is it easier to keep the same hero book after book?" he asked.

"As compared to what? I've only done it this way so I don't know. The challenging part is to bring John alive in every book without repeating previous books. Yet I have to give enough information that a person who didn't read earlier books can understand and know him as well as people who have read all the books in order."

"This is the third?"

Smiling gently, she shook her head. "The fifth. The third book just hit the bookstores. Book four will come out at Christmas and this one late next summer. I'm contracted to finish it by the end of next month, but I'm shooting to finish earlier."

He threw her a quick glance. "I'm ashamed to say I haven't read any of them." Writing was her livelihood. He should have taken at least a token interest in it. She had willingly helped him out of a tight spot when he'd asked her. Many nights he'd talked to her about the work in Kuwait.

She'd listened with every appearance of interest when she probably hadn't a clue to most of what he was talking about. She had always asked about his job, and he had never reciprocated.

The least he could have done was read one of her books, talked to her a bit about her writing. Maybe spent more time with her in Kuwait. She must have been lonely, yet she never complained. In fact, he couldn't remember ever hearing Trisha complain about anything. How did she stay so content?

For a moment an unexpected feeling of protectiveness and possession took hold. He wanted to protect her from his own rude behavior, his own ignorance of her writing, from the hurt she must feel that he had never inquired about it. He'd known her for years; she was almost another member of his family. For that reason alone he should have shown more interest in what she was doing.

And as his wife, he certainly should have shown some interest.

"Are they good?" he asked whimsically. He'd get a copy of one today and read it. Good or bad, he wanted to see how she wrote. Did she give away part of herself in the writing? Or was it all fiction? And why mysteries? She was such a feminine woman, he'd have expected romance novels.

"I think they're good. And people are buying them."

"Trisha, will you make enough to live on? I know writers don't make much money, unless they're some superstar bestselling author. Will you be able to manage once we separate?" That protectiveness reared up again. Had he made a mistake taking her from her job at the library? Would she be able to manage on her own?

"I'll manage. In fact—"

"You'd tell me, wouldn't you, if you need something, even after we're divorced?"

"I won't need anything."

"Except help in finding a husband." He frowned. The idea appealed less and less every time he thought about it.

"Oh, yes, except for that." She'd almost forgotten her ploy to learn what would attract him. And it obviously didn't matter to him; he was willing to indulge her. Probably glad to get her off his hands. The sun dimmed a little in the afternoon sky.

The house was closed up when they reached home. Trisha went ahead to open the door. Cole followed, carrying the computer.

"Your mother went to Becky's for the evening," Trisha said, reading the note Peggy had left on the counter.

"Probably didn't know when we would be home and wanted company. I know it's been a hard day for her." Cole walked through to the dining room and set the computer on the table. Two minutes later he placed the monitor and keyboard in place.

"Should we put it there?" Trisha asked from the doorway. "Won't I be in your mom's way?"

"Not as long as Dad's in the hospital. We'll eat in the kitchen, so this won't interfere. Sorry I don't have a separate office for you to use."

"This will be fine. It's what I used at home when I wrote the first book. And what I had in Kuwait." For a moment Trish remembered how she'd had to be available to rush to her father's bed if he called. The dining room had worked well both there and in their small apartment in Kuwait. When she returned to her house, she would turn one bedroom into an office.

"Since Mom's not here, what do you say to our going out to dinner?" Cole asked.

She glanced up, hesitated, then slowly smiled at his suggestion. "Perfect. A date—I can get started with my lessons."

He frowned. "Not a date, just going out to dinner."

"No, we must treat it like a date. I haven't dated in years. I hope I haven't forgotten how," she teased. Excitement built. She had never gone on a date with Cole. Would it be fun? Would he put himself out at all to see they had a good time, or was he just looking for a quick bite to eat before they headed to the hospital?

"People don't ever forget how to date. Your whole notion about practicing to entice some man is dumb. You're fine the way you are," he said gruffly.

"Why, Cole, how nice of you to say so. Thank you." Trisha turned and glanced provocatively at him over her shoulder. "I'll just need a few minutes to change into something more suitable for dinner. Are we going dancing, too?"

"No, we're going to get something to eat, that's all."

"Okay."

"I need to shower," he grumbled, following her up the steps to the second floor, watching her hips sway seductively beneath the short skirt she wore. Her waist nipped in above the flaring hips. He wanted to cup her bottom and feel the heat from her skin scorch his hand.

Her hair hung down her back in a clip. He wished he could reach out and unfasten it, run the silky tresses through his fingers, rub the soft waves against his face. If she didn't stop flaunting that sexy body, he would forget analyzing the different ramifications of a possible change in their relationship for the next few months and take her straight to bed.

"I knew that. You always shower as soon as you get home. I'll dress while you shower and wait for you downstairs." She grinned, thinking how this was the closest thing she had to a normal relationship with him since she'd known him.

He took a deep breath. Damn, he was getting hard again, just following her. He stormed into the bathroom. He hated cold showers, but at the rate his blood was heating, that would be the only way to go. When he stripped and stepped beneath the water, he gasped at the shock. He was not taking her on a date. They were just going out to have dinner. Maybe talk a little bit. She could tell him more about being a writer, about her books. He could tell her something about what he was finding at Langford Construction.

For someone not interested in dating, he suddenly began to plan where they could go that would give them a quiet dinner. He knew a couple of supper clubs where there was quiet dancing. He could hold her in his arms and move with her to the music.

Snapping off the water, he quickly dried himself, then wiped off the mirror. He had time for a quick shave. If this were to be a date, he wanted to end it right and kiss her good-night. He didn't want his late-afternoon beard to mar her sweet satiny skin.

Not that he was *planning* to kiss her, he thought as he lathered his cheeks, though if the opportunity arose, he wanted to be ready. Trisha's kisses were hot and heady. Too potent for her to be indiscriminate with them. He'd have to give her some gentle pointers if she was serious about this dating business. Other men might try to take advantage of her.

An uncomfortable emotion strangely like jealousy reared up. He didn't want to think of Trisha kissing other men. She was too innocent, too gentle. She needed someone to take care of her. Someone like him . . .

Five

Trisha listened when Cole began his shower. She flung off her skirt and shirt and grabbed a dressy sundress. It was warm enough even late in the evening to wear it. Pale yellow, it had narrow straps, a fitted bodice and a flared skirt that ended just above her knees. She donned strappy white sandals. Brushing out her hair, she sprayed a cloud of her favorite perfume and walked through it, shaking her hair so it would capture as much of the mist as possible. Then she French-braided it. A touch of makeup and she was ready. She really needed to go shopping. This dress was four years old, not at all the kind of seductive attire that would capture Cole's attention. And her hair was cool and neat in the braid, but hardly enticing. Would a shorter cut be more provocative?

She reached over to the notebook beside her bed, rereading some of the notations. She had left off "flirting at every opportunity." Well, almost every opportunity. She jotted it down. She needed the practice, if she could gird herself enough to try without feeling like a total idiot.

The shower had ended several minutes ago. She glanced around the room. Had Cole taken in a change of clothing, or would he have to come in here to dress? Would he put on his clothes if she were still there? For a daring moment she considered plopping down on the bed and waiting for him to come in. He'd seen her start to dress a couple of days ago. She'd like to return the favor.

But she shook her head. She didn't think she was up to that just yet.

Knocking on the bathroom door to let him know she was going downstairs, Trisha was startled when it instantly opened. Cole stood in the frame, a damp towel wrapped around his waist, his face lathered for shaving. Trisha caught her breath. His shoulders gleamed in the light, tanned and damp. His chest muscles were clearly defined, firm and supple beneath his taut skin, with a faint dusting of light hair between his flat nipples, drifting down in a wedge to slip beneath the draped towel. She swallowed hard, jerking her eyes back up to meet his.

"I—" She cleared her throat. "I'll wait for you downstairs. Um, you didn't have to shave."

"I wanted to. For later."

"Later?" Her heart beat faster.

"Kisses."

"Kisses?" She sounded like an echo.

"Kisses." Cole's gaze drifted down to her mouth.

Trisha licked suddenly dry lips, her own gaze mesmerized by the gleam in Cole's. She was unable to move, unable to think, envisioning the two of them locked in a warm embrace.

"Isn't that how dates end, with a good-night kiss?" he asked softly, reaching out to capture her chin in his fingers, brushing his thumb lightly across her lower lip.

"You said kisses."

"Yes." He smiled, his thumb brushing again.

It wasn't fair. She was about to melt under the intensity of his gaze, under the sensuous feel of his thumb. And he didn't appear the slightest bit affected. Her heart skidded, sped up, raced. Butterflies did a rumba in her stomach. Her skin glowed with the heat that flashed through her. And her active imagination provided an image of a kiss that practically had her swooning. She could hardly wait.

"Shall we skip dinner? Let me take you to bed, Trisha."

"I'll be down in about ten minutes." Cole shut the door in her face.

Slowly Trish turned and stumbled down the stairs, holding the railing to keep from falling, half-dazed as anticipation spread. He was planning to kiss her good-night! And not a single kiss, if he could be trusted. Kisses, he'd said.

Sex games. Was this the prelude to sex games with Cole? Would the kisses lead to much more? She stopped by the mirror in the hall to check her appearance. She looked fine, hair neat, color high in her cheeks, eyes sparkling in secret delight. She danced around in a circle, already wishing the evening was over and they were started on those kisses.

Unable to sit still, Trisha wandered out to the backyard to sit on the wooden bench swing that hung from the huge oak tree. The afternoon air was soft, warm, humid. The roses Peggy cherished were in full bloom, beautiful, colorful and fragrant. Pushing back in the swing, lifting her feet as it soared forward, Trisha kept her gaze on the back door. In only a few minutes her date would come out. She was finally going on a date with Cole Langford! And not just a casual date. But one that would end with them in bed together.

Now she had to figure out how to make sure sleep wasn't the only thing they did in that bed. She didn't want to learn how to entice other men. She only wanted to be able to entice this man. She had loved Cole for so long, somehow she should instinctively be able to reach through to him. Yet she felt uncertain. Was he doing this to merely humor her? Or was he serious about offering her pointers about dating? Would he calmly step aside and let her walk away, let her begin to date other men?

"You ready?" Cole called from the back door.

"Yes." Trisha sauntered across the yard to join him. He wore casual slacks and a sports jacket. She smiled at how handsome he looked. She would be the envy of all the women at the restaurant. "Should we write your mother a note, or call her at Becky's to let her know where we're going?"

"Yes, I'll call her and let her know where we'll be and that we'll go directly to the hospital from the restaurant."

Trisha waited beside him in the kitchen while he made the call. Fiddling with things on the counter, she kept her eyes on Cole, feasting on how wonderful he looked. Time and time again her eyes rested on his firm lips. She licked her own, remembering his taste from their earlier kiss. Remembering the promise he'd implied of future kisses when the night ended. She wished he'd step up to her now and—

Cole hung up the phone and turned to her. "Becky invited us for dinner, but I told her we already had plans. We'll go tomorrow night, all right?"

She nodded, moving her gaze lest he guess what she'd been thinking.

"Mom called the hospital and the reports are still good on Dad. He's expected to sleep through till morning, so I don't suppose there's any need to go to the hospital tonight."

She shook her head.

"We can go eat, then swing by and pick Mom up from Becky's and bring her home when we come home."

She nodded.

"Trisha, stop talking so much."

Smiling self-consciously, she met his eyes and shrugged.

Cole leaned over and brushed his lips against hers. Instantly Trisha opened her mouth, longing for more than a quick caress. She wanted to feel the heat and hunger from that morning. Wanted to assuage her own hunger for Cole, as if she ever could.

He lifted his head a scant inch and gazed down at her up-turned face. Trisha knew her expression showed the desire and love that flooded her, but she couldn't help it.

"Do you want to go eat, or stay here?" he asked softly, his breath mingling with hers. His lips mere millimeters from hers.

Stay here! Stay here! she wanted to scream. But she took a breath, too uncertain to give in to the urges that were al-most overwhelming. "Eat," she lied.

He sighed and straightened.

"We'll come back here," Trisha said, wishing she had answered differently. "After our date."

"We need to talk about that," he said as they headed for the car. "You want to be careful getting entangled with anyone. Take your time. It'll take a while to get a divorce, once we start the process. You shouldn't rush right out and latch on to some man."

"I've enjoyed being married to you, Cole," Trisha said stiffly as he helped her into the car. "I told you, I like being part of a couple. And I want a family. If I don't want to be too old, I need to find a mate soon, don't you think?"

He slammed the door, rocking the car. She quietly fas-tened her seat belt as her eyes tracked his progress around the front of the vehicle. Interesting.

"Mama Celia's suit you?" he asked when he got behind the wheel.

"Sounds good." She would be the perfect date, agree-able and interested in what he had to say. And make it clear she was ready for a good-night kiss—and maybe more—when they got home!

Cole took them to the quiet restaurant near Waterside. They were given a small booth near the wall of windows that offered a perfect view of the marina. The sun rode low in the sky, glittering on the smooth water. The dining room was not crowded. The service was excellent and before long their food was brought piping hot from the kitchen.

"To your dad's speedy recovery," Trisha proposed when Cole filled her wineglass.

"To Dad." He touched the rim of his to hers and then sipped.

"Can you pull the company out of its problems?" she asked as she began to eat the Maryland crab cakes.

"Yes, I think so. It'll take some tight management. I wish I knew why he let things slide for so long."

"You don't think it was that he lost heart when you left for Kuwait, do you?" she asked, tilting her head as she waited for his response. It had been something she'd wondered about. Becky's letters had indicated her father's general lack of interest in things once Cole had left.

Cole looked startled. "I would never have thought so."

She shrugged. "Just an idea. I know from Becky that your dad was very disappointed that you didn't turn to him when you had the problem with Diane."

"He offered help, but I wanted to make it on my own." Cole didn't want to discuss the situation. It was over. He'd been a fool, but he'd learned from the event and wouldn't make the same mistake a second time.

"I'm sure he was proud of you for wanting to make it on your own, but he also wanted to help. You're his son. He hurt for you, wanted to do something to ease your pain." Trisha caught his eye. "Sometimes it's harder to take help than give it."

Cole nodded.

"Did you prove what you needed to prove?" she asked.

"That I can handle things myself?"

"Is that what you wanted to prove?"

Cole was silent so long Trisha thought he wasn't going to answer. Finally he spoke.

"I guess I felt pretty raw after Diane. I felt foolish. I should have known what she was doing, should have been able to help her stop the gambling. Should have recognized the signs she was interested in someone else. But the business needed so much attention. I didn't have time—"

"I don't think it was that, Cole. Usually people with problems like Diane have to want help first. And people have been betraying spouses for years. Don't let it destroy the rest of your life."

"It's not destroyed. I know what to watch for now, what to guard against. I needed to take control of my life and find my own way out of the mess. Dad wanted me to come back into the business, but all I could see was a handout to a son who had failed."

"Oh, Cole, I'm sure he didn't mean it that way. He just wanted to help you. He loves you, you're his only son. Don't you want to help him now when he needs it?"

"That's different."

Trisha remained silent, watching him carefully. There wasn't much difference in the two situations, but if Cole felt better about it the way it was, she wouldn't interfere.

"It worked out, Trisha. Thanks to you. I was able to pay off the rest of the debt and still have a few thousand dollars in the bank. Not enough to get started again, but I'm a lot closer."

"Maybe you should buy into your dad's business. Maybe you two could reach a compromise about what you want to build and complement each other, rather than clash all the time," she suggested softly.

He nodded. "Maybe. It's funny you said that. It's something I've been thinking about the past couple of days. Maybe we could make it work this time."

His eyes caught her gaze and held it. Trisha shivered as she felt the intensity to her soul. Dare she pursue it further, dare she try to get him to commit not only to trying a compromise with his father, but to continuing their marriage?

"Your dad will be in the hospital for another week or so, then will need some extra care at home. By the time he and your mother are ready to be on their own, my house will be vacant. I spoke to the Realtor today and told him to give my tenants notice to vacate. We have a month-to-month agreement." She held her breath. Would he still move in with her? Was he still planning to let their marriage continue?

Cole hesitated, drawing out the moment while he finished the last of the steak he'd ordered.

"Part of our agreement was that I would support you while we were married."

"But the house is paid for, so our living expenses would be very small. It would make it easier for you to get on your feet like we originally planned. And I'm making money on my books now, so—"

"You'll need to build up a backlog to carry you through between royalty checks. I know writers don't make much money. You need to be frugal to make sure you can support yourself once we separate."

If we separate, she thought, her gaze never leaving his.

"I'm doing all right."

"Good, that means you'll do even better down the road." He reached for her fingers, twining his with them. They could coast along for a few months, see how things went. He wanted to make sure Trisha would be able to support herself. She had expected to be supported for three years, had given up her job with that in mind. He had an obligation to make sure she was ready to be on her own before separating.

"If you want to start divorce proceedings as soon as your dad is home, I'll understand," she said, her eyes wide as she stared at him. If he said yes, could she pretend she didn't care? Or would she disgrace herself and beg him to reconsider?

"There's no rush."

"Not on my part. I thought on yours."

"No." He damn well didn't like the idea of her on the prowl for another man. They got on fine. There was no rush to separate.

Trisha fiddled with her water glass. She should tell him she was doing well with her books. She felt dishonest. She should let him know she no longer needed to depend on him for her livelihood. Yet she could live with the small deception if it kept Cole from moving on.

"Dinner was delicious," she said, smiling brightly. The soft strains of the music drifted in from the next room. "I'm having fun on our date. It's odd, isn't it? Most people date, then marry. We married and now are dating and discussing a divorce."

"We just decided not to discuss the divorce. Maybe later, when things are more settled." When he was more ready to let her go. When he didn't think about taking her to bed and capturing that heat that flared between them whenever they touched. When he didn't crave her touch, crave her mouth and hands and body. Maybe then he'd be ready to talk divorce.

"Will you dance with me?" she asked.

Cole nodded and rose, reaching out to take her hand in his as he led her into the bar. The dance floor was small; only two other couples took advantage of the music. He pulled her into his arms, settling her against his chest, encircling her with his strong arms.

Trisha sighed softly and snuggled against him. She reached her arms up to his shoulders, one resting on the sleek muscles there, the other tangling gently with the thick pelt of hair at the back of his head. She could feel him press against every inch of her, his muscular chest, strong legs. Leaning back slightly against the strong arms that held her so securely, she gazed up into his narrowed eyes.

"This is nice," she said softly. "Should I expect evenings like this with all my dates?"

A muscle jerked in his cheek as he dropped his face closer to hers. "You're pushing your luck, lady. Dancing like this should be only with a man you know very, very well." Lightly brushing his lips against hers, he tucked her head against his neck and dropped one hand to the swell of her hips, hauling her in closer.

Almost unable to move for the shimmering sensations that swept through her, Trisha smiled and leaned against Cole, grateful for the opportunity to be in his arms, if only for a dance.

The music segued from one romantic song into another, each one slower and dreamier than the previous. On and on they circled the dance floor, lost in a world of senses—touch and sway and soft, soft music. The dim light cocooned them in a world of their own.

Cole knew they should leave. He should pay the bill and drive them to Becky's to pick up his mother. He needed to get out of here. Put her away from him and gain some perspective. But he couldn't let go. He didn't want to end their evening. Trisha felt like heaven in his arms. Her light fragrance surrounded him. The sweet seductive curves of her body enticed him. It was all he could do to control his hands and keep them on her back when he really wanted to find a dark place and strip her until he could roam over every inch of her luscious body. He wanted kisses to heat the night. He wanted her to call his name with passion and give herself to him in the most basic, primal manner.

He couldn't take much more before he lost control completely. When the song ended, he took her arm and steered her from the dance floor.

"Come on, we have to get Mom."

Trisha blinked, the dreamy mood shattered. What had happened? She could scarcely think, her emotions and feelings had been so totally caught up in Cole's embrace, in the imagination she fed so fervently of them hurrying home and into their room. She wanted him, and to be so close was torture.

"It's not that late," she protested as he hurried her to the parking lot. "Just after ten."

"Mom will be wondering where we are."

"I hope all my dates don't have to rush home to Mother," she said petulantly.

"Will you shut up about dates? You're a married woman and I'm your husband. I sure as hell don't want to hear about dates."

Turning away lest he see her sudden smile, Trisha's heart danced with unexpected happiness. It bothered him to talk about her dating. That had to mean he wasn't as indifferent to her as he tried to pretend.

Afraid to say something that would spoil the evening, Trisha remained silent until they reached Becky's place. Peggy was waiting to leave. She and Trisha spoke of their day while Cole drove. In no time they were back home.

Peggy immediately declared herself exhausted and excused herself to go to bed. Trisha bade her mother-in-law good-night and slowly turned to Cole.

"Is our evening over?" she asked softly.

He waited until he heard his mother's door close, then moved to draw Trisha into his arms. "Do you want it to be over?"

Daringly she brushed her fingers against his smooth cheek, tracing the strong line of his jaw with her index finger. "Actually, I thought you had shaved in case we wanted to exchange a good-night kiss. I would hate for that to have been done in vain."

With a soft groan he pulled her closer and covered her mouth with his. His lips were firm and hot and teased hers. Nibbling on her lower lip, his tongue licked the corner of her mouth. When Trisha moved her head, he trailed wet kisses along her cheek, her jaw. Back to her lips, he kissed her long and hard.

Almost frantic with the roiling sensations that lapped through every inch of her body, Trisha tried to capture his mouth, to deepen the kiss. But he wouldn't let her. He trailed quick kisses down her neck, focused on the pulse point at the base of her throat, stroking it with his tongue, sucking lightly with his lips.

She shivered beneath his touch, yearning for more. Startled, she realized the soft cries echoing around them were her own. She threaded her fingers in his hair and tried to pull his face to hers. He allowed it.

Fastening her lips to his, she slipped her tongue along his lips, past the barrier of his strong teeth, to the dark cavern of his mouth. It felt like coming home. Slowly Trisha deepened the kiss, reveling in the pleasure she found in his arms, in his mouth. When he pushed back into her own mouth, she retreated, mating her tongue with his.

He tasted of desire and heat and Cole. She couldn't get enough. She felt the pounding beat of her heart, the gasping of breath as she fought for air. But she didn't want to stop, she wanted to continue in his arms forever.

Suddenly he broke the kiss and tipped her head back. Reluctantly Trisha opened her eyes, afraid of what she might see.

"Let me tell you something about dating," Cole said, breathing heavily. His fingers moved to the back of her head, unfastened the clip that held her braid and began to release the strands. "Nothing will drive a man crazier than hair that cries out to be released and mussed." When the last plait had been released, he combed his fingers through the wavy mass. Again and again he lifted her hair, separating strands with his fingers, rubbing the tresses between his thumb and fingers. He took a handful and brought it around to rub against his cheek, slowly, as if savoring every glossy strand.

He never took his eyes from hers.

Trisha felt desire blossom deep inside, swell and sweep through her like a blowtorch. She had never felt anything so erotic. They were linked by the band of hair that he continued to rub against his skin, by the gazes locked together, by the clamoring bodies that wanted more.

"So I should leave it hanging down in the future, not put it up?" she asked, mesmerized by the deep gleam in his silvery eyes.

"I didn't say that. When it hangs down it swirls around when you shake your head, crying out for a man's fist to wrap the silky length around it."

"What then, get it cut?"

"No!" The word was harsh. "Don't get it cut."

"But if putting it up causes problems and letting it hang down causes problems, what should I do?" She moved closer, tilting her head back to invite another kiss. Slowly she traced her lower lip with her tongue, her eyes daring him to refuse her blatant invitation.

"You have a dilemma, baby," he said real low as he ignored the dare and closed his mouth over hers again.

He drew his hands up her bare arms, to the thin straps of her dress. Slowly slipping his fingers beneath the material, he rubbed back and forth gently. She was so soft, her skin smooth and warm. He liked touching her, enjoying the difference in their skin. He wanted to touch every inch of her, from the silky texture of her breasts to the warmth and heat of her most secret part. He wanted Trisha like he'd never wanted any other woman, not even Diane.

With the thought came jarring reality. Cole pulled back, pushing Trisha away to hold at arm's length.

She looked puzzled. "Is something wrong?" Her face was flushed, her lips rosy and slightly swollen. Her hair was tousled around her shoulders as if she'd just come from bed. She looked gorgeous.

"Nothing's wrong. Time to stop, is all." Cole dropped his hands, turned away.

"Time to stop? Why?" Anger flared. Who was he to say it was time to stop? Was this just some kind of brief interlude for him to while away a few minutes? Had he any idea how arousing his kisses were? How inflaming his touch was? Didn't he have any idea how much she wanted him?

"The next thing you know, we'll get carried away."

She put her hands on her hips, allowing some of her anger to spill over. "Excuse me, but weren't you the one who suggested sex games? What's the problem here? Changed your mind?" It was anger or tears. For a moment Trisha wasn't sure which would win.

"Calm down. I haven't changed my mind. But I want us to have a chance to think things through. It's easy to get caught up in the heat of passion. I don't want you doing something that you'll regret later. Sex between us can only complicate things."

"I'm not so sure. They seem pretty complicated to me right now." Trisha turned and ran up the steps. She wished she could slam the door behind her to let him know how angry she was, but that would wake Peggy. She grabbed his pillow from the bed and threw it against the door. She was so mad she could spit. She had touched heaven tonight in his arms, and he thought it complicated things.

She'd show him complicated. She'd get him so tied up in knots he wouldn't know which way was up. How dare he stop them! Unless . . . unless he hadn't been as caught up in the moment as she had been.

She sank onto the bed. She didn't think that was the case. He'd seemed pretty involved to her. But what did she know? Sex was not an area in which she considered herself an expert. Any more than she was in knowing how to seduce him. Dressing before him had no effect. Her kisses, while nice, she was sure, certainly didn't drive him wild. She closed her eyes in anguish. Couldn't she attract him? Was there nothing there for him to come to love?

"No, by God. I'll find a way!"

She stood to take off her dress. She'd pursue him until he filed for divorce. She'd be the most loving wife he ever saw, and only if he flat out told her to get lost would she leave. Otherwise she was sticking to him like glue to paper.

Or a lover to a lover.

Slipping beneath the sheet, she turned out the light, wondering if he planned to come up to bed tonight. Wondering what she could do that would make him see her as a possible mate for life. He didn't like her idea of dating other men. Was that a start? Did that mean he wanted her for himself? What could she do to make him admit that?

Six

Trisha lay awake, counting the minutes. What was Cole doing? She'd come upstairs a half hour ago. Wasn't he planning to come to bed tonight? He could easily sleep downstairs on the sofa. As long as he awakened before his mother, she'd never know, never suspect her son was anything but happily married.

Which he could be, if he only knew it, Trisha repeated softly to herself. They had been happy in Kuwait. Or at least content. And she was nothing like Diane. Why couldn't he see that? Why couldn't he let himself relax and enjoy what they had between them, let himself envision a future with her? Give love a chance to grow?

The minutes slowly ticked by. She wasn't the slightest bit tired. Her body still hummed from the hot kisses and caresses they'd shared in the kitchen. She wanted more. She ached for the magic of his touch. Lightly her tongue traced her lips, tasting him again. Reaching out, she let her hand brush over the mattress where he slept. No matter how hard she tried, she couldn't imagine him there; she needed the reality of his presence. Nothing else would satisfy.

Sighing, she turned over on her side. At this rate it would be dawn before she slept. Had he decided to sleep downstairs? Dare she go to find out? Just then she heard Cole's tread on the steps. He was coming up after all. Relief washed through her. Her heart rate sped up in delicious anticipation. Holding her breath, she strained to listen. When the door opened, she closed her eyes, pretending sleep. She didn't want him to know she'd stayed awake waiting for him. Let him think she hadn't a care in the world and that his kisses hadn't been the most wonderful thing that ever happened to her. She had a certain amount of pride, didn't she?

She heard every move he made. She knew when he shed his shirt and tossed it over the chair. She heard the rasp of his zipper, and heat flushed through her as she recalled the sculpted planes of his hard, muscular body. She wished she dared turn on the light. Wished she dared let her eyes trace the golden tanned skin from his broad shoulders to his washboard belly, to his taut thighs. She breathed in and out, counting the seconds, trying desperately to keep her breathing even and deep. She gripped the sheet beneath her hand.

The bed dipped when he climbed in. The air against her skin cooled as he lifted the sheet to slide beneath it. Then he settled on his pillow.

Trisha concentrated on breathing, her nerves at full alert. Her body tingled as she felt him near, felt his warmth, felt his presence fill the room. And her yearning grew.

She almost stopped breathing when an idea flashed into her mind. It was brilliant, even if she did say so herself. Slowly she opened her eyes to determine how dark it was. Black as pitch—perfect. With a soft sigh and slow stretch, she rolled over until she ran into Cole. Slowly she snuggled up against him, letting one leg cross his, letting her arm slowly encircle his chest. She forced her breathing to remain even and hoped to goodness he couldn't feel the rapid beat of her heart. She didn't want him to know she was awake—he might reject her, feel duty-bound to push her away.

"God, baby, you're going to be the death of me," Cole said softly, gathering her up into his arms, resting her head against his shoulder, his hands moving to slip beneath the loose T-shirt to find a warm spot against her bare skin. He rested his cheek against the top of her head, his soft breath skimming her hair. She was hot and sweet and he wanted nothing more than to roll her over on her back and make love to her all night long.

But he'd been doing some serious thinking downstairs. A year ago everything had seemed so clear-cut. He'd marry Trisha, they'd go to Kuwait for three years. When they returned, they'd separate. Now that plan was shot to bits, and he couldn't seem to formulate a replacement.

She had every reason to expect him to support her for three years. That had been the original plan. But it had also been his intention to keep their relationship purely platonic. That had been blown away when they were forced to share a bed.

For a year he'd done his best to ignore the compelling femininity of his wife. To be married to a woman and have to keep his distance had not been easy, but he'd done it. There had been work enough to keep him occupied until he was too tired to do anything but sleep.

The fact that they had to share a bed wasn't the only change. Trisha herself had changed. She'd been so circumspect in Kuwait. He almost didn't recognize her here. Gone was the cool, collected wife who had shared his apartment. In her place was a warm vibrant woman who looked at him with flirtatious provocation. Who responded to his kisses with ones so hot and potent he had trouble remembering his name. Had he just wasted a year?

They needed to talk about the future. Maybe they should continue with the original plan. If he stayed with her at her home, two more years would ensure he could save enough to get back into the business, either on his own or in partnership with his father. It would also ensure that Trisha would have a chance to build up some reserves. The last thing he wanted to do was threaten her livelihood. But he didn't like depending on her cooperation to make it all work. He still didn't like depending on anyone.

He sighed. He'd have to think about it some more.

Trisha smelled the brandy on his breath and it surprised her. They had not had spirits of any kind in Kuwait. Since returning home, they had not had anything beyond wine. Why the need for brandy? Immediately following that thought, she wondered what he would taste like now. Her hand rested on his strong chest, the hair beneath crinkly. She wanted to drag her fingers through, trace every inch, see if he reacted as she did if she brushed his nipples. She longed to reach up and capture his mouth, let her tongue brush against his lips, taste him and brandy. But she held herself still. It was torture. This had definitely not been one of her brighter ideas. How long could she pretend to be asleep when every nerve ending in her body craved his touch so much she almost trembled with need?

His hot hand at her waist was distracting, but the hand that rested on her bottom was the one that was driving her crazy. He had only to move it a few inches and— She swallowed and tried to think of something else. She'd blow the whole thing by giving in to the wanton pictures that danced in her brain—the two of them face to face, breast to chest, hip to hip, on the bed, making glorious hot love.

"Go to sleep, Trisha," he said ever so softly.

She froze. He knew she was awake. Embarrassed, she pushed away, only to have his arms tighten and hold her in place.

"We've slept like this the last couple of nights, we can do it again. Go to sleep." His voice was a rough, husky growl.

She tried to relax. It felt right to be in his arms. She wanted more, but for tonight she had this. He hadn't pushed her away. Slowly her heart rate returned to normal. Slowly the tension slipped away. Slowly she felt herself falling asleep.

Trisha awoke the next morning nestled against Cole. Her back was against his chest, his thighs rested beneath hers. His hand cupped one breast. His breath brushed against her neck as he breathed deeply. She felt his arousal against her bottom. Instantly aware of him as never before, she wondered what she should do.

To turn around and kiss him offered the most daring choice. She didn't think she could pull that off. But she didn't want to leave the bed until he awoke. For a little while she could cherish the feelings that rushed through her. Savor this special time with Cole.

"Awake?" he asked softly. His hand tightened slightly on her breast, released as his fingers traced across her heated skin.

"Yes. Why do I bother to wear a T-shirt to bed?" she asked grumpily, remembering last night and the other morning. He easily found her bare skin; she should give up trying for modesty.

He chuckled. "I've wondered that myself. Maybe you should go back to sleeping in the nude as you say you normally do. It would save time."

"Save time?" She rolled over onto her back, looking up at him.

"Yeah, all the seconds it's going to take to pull the shirt over your head." He bunched the soft cotton up around her neck, exposing her breasts to the warmth of his gaze, to the coolness of the early-morning air.

"Have you always been this pretty, or is it a recent thing?" he asked, moving his gaze to her slumberous eyes. His hand was hot on her ribs, just below her breasts. She lay perfectly still, drifting on the sensations, wondering if he would move up just a few scant inches...

She smiled her pleasure at his compliment. "What do you think?" My God, was that sultry voice hers? Was she actually flirting with him?

"I think I've been blind. All these years I've only seen you as Becky's friend."

"And now?"

"And now I—"

"Cole? Are you and Trisha awake? I have hotcakes ready for the griddle. I want to get to the hospital early to be there when your father wakes up," Peggy's voice called up the stairs.

"Okay, Mom, we'll be down in a couple of minutes," he replied, holding Trisha's gaze.

She lowered her lids to hide her disappointment. Yanking down her shirt, she rolled over and pushed back the sheet to get out of bed.

"Trish?"

"I'll only be a couple of minutes in the bathroom, then it'll be all yours." Avoiding his eyes, she snatched up some clothes and hurried across the hall. Closing the door behind her, she leaned against it for a long moment. They had been so close! Blast, it wasn't fair!

Trisha regained her normally cheery disposition by the time she finished dressing and went downstairs to help Peggy with breakfast. She glanced at Cole when he joined them, but saw no trace of disappointment or regret that they'd been interrupted. For a moment her equilibrium faltered, then righted itself. Why should he feel anything but a mild annoyance that they didn't get to do more than talk this morning? He wasn't in love with her. She had better do her best to act unconcerned. She refused to let him know how she felt. She still remembered the laughter when she'd been a teenager. She couldn't bear that now.

When they reached the hospital, Cole gave Trisha the keys to the car.

"You drive Mom home when she wants to go. I'm going to check on Dad, then head for the site. I'll borrow one of the company pickup trucks to use until we get a car of our own."

"Do you want me to drive you there?"

"No, I called Ben at work. He'll pick me up. Stay with Mom as long as she needs you, will you?"

Trisha nodded.

"I don't need anyone to baby-sit me, Cole. Once Trisha sees Matt, she can go on home and work on her book if she needs to. I'm planning to stay all day. I brought my knitting and a book to read. Just pick me up in time for dinner," his mother said.

"What time did Becky say to be there?"

"Around six-thirty."

"Okay, I'll go home and shower after work. Then Trisha and I will swing by here to pick you up," Cole said. "That suit you, Trish?"

She nodded.

He smiled again and leaned closer. "Chatty again?"

She looked at those lips, remembering last night. Her eyes dancing, she glanced up to meet his. And nodded.

He chuckled and flung his arm around her shoulder. "Go check Dad, Mom. He'll be anxious to see you."

"You should go first since you have to leave for the site."

"No, I can wait. It's more important for him to see his wife first. Just don't stay all day."

She smiled and hurried down the hall.

"I can give you a ride to the site," Trisha said as Cole led her into the waiting room. It was deserted.

"No need. Ben and I have things we can discuss on the ride over. I'll be home before six."

"Okay."

He paused near the window and glanced over his shoulder. Seeing no one around, he turned Trisha around and kissed her gently.

"Didn't get a chance to do that earlier." His husky voice splashed through her like heated wine. She smiled and shook her head. The unexpected kiss made up for some of her earlier disappointment.

He kissed her again and again—light, sipping kisses. A mere touching of lips to lips, to cheeks, to forehead. Back to lips, he deepened the kiss slightly. Always aware of where they were and that they might be interrupted at any moment, Cole made sure the embrace didn't get out of hand. But he wanted to kiss her. Always a man to go after what he wanted, he saw no reason to deny himself this morning. She tasted sweet. He wished he had awakened earlier this morning, long before his mother had. Even now he could feel the heat of Trisha's body mingling with his.

"Mmm," Trisha murmured.

"Mmm?" Cole repeated, resting his forehead against hers and gazing down into her pretty brown eyes.

"Nice."

More than nice. Let's head back home when we see Dad. We'll have the house to ourselves and can take up where Mom interrupted this morning.

"Mmm. But I've got to get to work and if we don't stop, I won't be able to walk."

She blinked at that, then giggled softly. One day she would stop wishing he would say what she wanted to hear and accept things the way they were. "We can't have that now, can we? I only wish your mom hadn't gotten up so early this morning." She toyed with the button at the top of his shirt.

"Doesn't matter. We didn't have much time this morning anyway. Your first time should be at night when we would have hours to enjoy ourselves, not a hurried coupling before breakfast."

She blinked, the sudden knowledge Cole was thinking of making love to her almost overshadowed by what he'd said. "You mean our first time together, don't you?"

He pulled back to better see her, his eyes narrowed.

"Cole, I'm twenty-seven years old. You didn't expect me to still be a virgin, did you?" A touch of surprise pressed against her. From the dull color that scored his cheeks she knew he had expected exactly that. Would it matter?

"I guess I did think…" he said, looking away, feeling like a total idiot. Of course she had had lovers before. She was a pretty, sexy, exciting woman to whom men would be instinctively attracted. What a fool he'd been to suspect otherwise.

"Does it make a difference that I'm not? I mean, were you a virgin when you married Diane? Have you been totally celibate since then?" A touch of fear clutched at her. It couldn't matter. Not in this day and age. It wasn't as if she were promiscuous. It had only been that one time. On the occasion of Cole's wedding to Diane.

He smiled sardonically. "I haven't slept with a woman since Diane, but you're right, I wasn't a virgin on that wedding day any more than either of us was when we married. My mistake. From what Becky said, I had the impression you didn't date. From that I guess I assumed that you never had, or at least not enough to—"

"I didn't date much. It was in college." She could explain further, but wouldn't. He could take a flying leap off a tall building if it made any difference. She turned away, tears threatening. She couldn't explain why, either. She had had years to get over the regret of sleeping with Bobby just to try to forget Cole, to forget that the man she had loved for years was marrying another woman. It hadn't worked. She had broken off with Bobby and not tried it again, but she wasn't about to explain herself to Cole.

He came up behind her and folded her in his arms, crossing them beneath her breasts, his head coming beside hers.

"It doesn't make a bit of difference. You just caught me by surprise, that's all. That's one of the reasons I've held back. I didn't want to do anything irrevocable when we have only a temporary marriage."

Temporary marriage. He had started this marriage that way and saw it in those terms only. She sighed. Was she fighting a useless battle? Could she get him to change his mind?

"It was a long time ago. I was just twenty-one," she said softly.

"And not since then? Honey, you're a pretty woman. What are the men thinking of?"

She shrugged, as much as she could in his embrace. "Some of it's me. I didn't want to do it again."

"Why not?"

"It's nothing to write home about," she said waspishly, trying to pull away from his embrace. His arms only tightened.

He chuckled. "It can be."

With the right man, yes, she thought, *it might be.* But would she ever get to try with the right man? With Cole?

"There you two are. Matt's awake, though still numb and groggy with all the painkillers. Go on in and see him, Cole. I'll go back after you and Trisha have a chance to visit with him." Peggy bustled into the waiting room, her face bright and relaxed after satisfying herself that her husband was doing all right.

Cole released his wife and turned without another word to head down the hall. He was floored at his reaction when he learned Trisha had slept with someone. Anger and jealousy had surged through him as if she were his private property. He really had no reason to suspect she was still a virgin at her age, but he had. And he'd thought a lot last night about initiating her into the rites of lovemaking. Now someone else had beat him to it.

The feelings didn't fade, even though he had no reason to feel that way. It was totally ridiculous. They had married for convenience. *His* convenience. When the need was gone, they would get a quiet divorce and go their separate ways. He had no hold on Trisha, nor did she owe him any loyalty beyond the terms of their marriage.

Even now she was thinking of finding another husband. The anger turned up a notch. She didn't need to rush into anything. Maybe they would stay married the full three years. He could see advantages to it. Maybe if they made love, Trisha would be more content. Maybe she wouldn't want to rush out and find some other man to love. After all, they'd done well in Kuwait, sharing interests in common, enjoying the same activities.

He took a deep breath and pushed open the door to his father's room. Time enough later to think of the problem with his wife. He had a job to do to help out his father. One problem at a time.

Ten minutes later Cole left his father's room at the request of the nurse who wanted to run some tests. He leaned casually against the wall beside the door, waiting until he could go back inside. It was disturbing to see his father laid low like that. All his life his dad had seemed like such a strong, invincible force. This heart attack and operation had shown Cole that his father was a man like any other, susceptible to the same illnesses and limitations. And his father needed him now. Needed to be able to count on him, depend on his strength. It was payback time and Cole was ready and able, and glad for the opportunity.

A movement down the hall caught his attention. Trisha was walking toward the room. He watched her draw closer, a honey-sweet baby he wanted to clasp in his arms and never let go. Her walk was sultry and sexy, yet she hadn't a clue. Her wide-eyed innocence grabbed a man's heart and wouldn't turn it loose. She'd hung on his every word last night, making him feel like a giant. She'd poured herself into their kisses, until he thought he'd explode. If he'd known last night what he now knew, would he have called a halt to their lovemaking? He didn't think so.

Pushing away from the wall, he walked to meet her.

"Is Matt all right?" she asked, peering toward his father's room.

"The nurse is with him." Cole reached out and took her arm, pulling her around to the wall, leaning over her, resting his forearm on the cool tile, sheltering her from anyone who happened to glance down the wide hallway.

"Did you want me to go back to the waiting room?" she asked breathlessly. Every time she was close to him she had trouble with her breathing. She tightened her hands into fists to keep from reaching out to touch him, to link herself with him, however tenuously.

"What I want to do is find an empty room somewhere and close the door behind us. Then I want to draw the blinds and make the room dark and quiet." Slowly he let his fingers toy with the top button of her shirt, releasing it from its hole. "Then I want to put you on a high hospital bed and crawl in with you and play doctor until neither one of us can stand." His clever fingers released another button.

Trish ignored the warning cries in her mind and reached out her fingers to slip them between the buttons of his work shirt, rubbing against the heated flesh she found. Tugging gently against the body hair, she smiled as he sucked in his breath in reaction.

"You do, do you?" she asked huskily, tilting her head up to meet his hot gaze. "What about work?"

"Forget work." His fingers skimmed across her collarbone, leaving icy fire in their wake. He eased his hand beneath the collar of the shirt, massaging her shoulder muscles.

"Your friend Ben is in the waiting room. Should we tell him first, or let him search for us when you don't show?" She wet her top lip deliberately with her tongue, her eyes holding his as she flirted with danger.

"Keep that up and I'll dump somebody out of a bed, send them to X-ray or something. I won't be able to wait until we find an empty room."

"Talk is cheap, Cole. You've got to go to work."

He leaned against her, pressing her back into the cool tile wall. Both arms leaned against the wall, imprisoning her in the confines of his body. "I'm the boss. I can take a day off."

"You just got here."

He bent his head and met her waiting lips, covering them, searching for the hot-honey warmth of her with his lips and tongue. She arched against him, pushing away from the wall, straining to meet the flare of passion that rose at his touch.

The soft chiming of the hospital intercom brought them back to reality. Down the hall a nurse pushed a cart. Trisha broke the kiss by turning her head and pushing against his chest. He stepped back.

"Go see Ben," Trisha said softly, her hand lingering on his chest as if reluctant to break contact.

Cole ran his fingers through his hair and stared down at her. He wanted her in the worst way, more than he'd wanted any woman before. She was pretty, sexy and exuded such an air of innocence. Yet her responses to his kisses were anything but innocent. She had fiery depths he wanted to plumb. She had a look about her that heated his blood until he thought he'd burn up. And soon he was going to do just that, with her. Burn them both up.

"Until later, then."

She nodded, finally drawing her hand away. "You can count on it," she said.

Trisha watched him walk away, wanting to dance for joy in the hallway. He wanted her, that was clear. After all these years, he wanted her. For a night, a week, however long, she would relish every single second with him. It was so much more than she'd ever thought she'd have. Yet it was still less than what she wanted.

She wanted it all. One way or another, she was going to try to get it!

It was hot. As Trisha loosened the angel food cake from the pan, she wondered for the tenth time in ten minutes why Peggy and Matt had never put in central air-conditioning. Virginia was notorious for its humid summers. The window units in the bedrooms made sleeping comfortable, but the kitchen needed one more than any other room. Especially when baking.

She dusted off the crumbs and studied the cake. She should have been writing. But she couldn't concentrate. Instead of the computer screen, she saw Cole. Instead of correcting the dialogue of her hero, she heard Cole's sexy voice suggesting they find an empty hospital bed. Closing her eyes, she remembered how she felt with his hands on her that morning. She was slowly going crazy. Crazy with longings and rising desire.

Hoping that baking would give her something else to think about, she'd decided to make a cake to take to Becky's tonight.

Now she was ready to frost the angel food cake with strawberries in whipped cream. The frosting was light, just a bit sweet and a perfect complement to the cake. They'd have to keep it in the cooler to take to Becky's. She hoped it wasn't too hot for the cream to whip.

She brushed her forehead with her arm. Drawing the chilled bowl and beaters from the refrigerator, she mashed the strawberries. Taking the heavy cream out, she began to whip it. The drone of the mixer filled the air as she slowly turned the bowl. It was getting close to six o'clock. Cole would be home soon. She still had to change her clothes before she was ready. The old shorts and skimpy top she wore would not do at all for dinner at Becky's. But it was the coolest thing she had for work in the hot kitchen.

She had pinned up her hair to keep it from getting in her way. It was damp with the heat. The soft scooped-neck top buttoned up the front, and she'd left a few buttons undone top and bottom to permit maximum circulation of any air that might be stirring. Did Peggy have a fan somewhere? If she did much more cooking, she'd invest in one.

She dipped her finger into the bowl, tasted the whipped cream. It was thick enough for the strawberries. She added some, mixed them in. Just about—

The hand on her shoulder scared her half to death. With a shriek, Trisha whirled around, pulling the mixer from the bowl, splattering whipped cream and strawberries on everything within five feet.

"Cole! My God, you scared me half to death!" Quickly she snapped off the mixer, looked in dismay at the mess on the counter, the wall, Cole, herself.

He grinned. "I called to you when I walked in, but I guess you didn't hear me."

"I certainly didn't. Look at this mess. I don't have time for this!" She slammed the mixer on the counter and reached for a damp dishcloth.

He reached out and stopped her, turning her around until she faced him. "I'm sorry. I thought you heard me." He studied her face for a long moment, his eyes locking with hers. "You have whipped cream here." He touched the corner of her mouth. Leaning over, he licked the cream off.

Trisha's anger changed to another emotion entirely. She felt his tongue brush across her skin, tasting her, tasting the strawberries and cream. Her heart skidded in her chest.

"You have some here." He licked her cheek. She was flushed from the heat in the kitchen, her scent mingled with that of the freshly baked cake and the sweet strawberries in the cream. He brought his hands up to hold her shoulders as he traced his tongue across her cheek, licking every splash of the whipped cream.

"Cole..." she whispered, her eyes closed as she enjoyed the exquisite sensations jostling through her. He needed to stop before she was a quivering mass of nerves and cravings. But she couldn't tell him that.

"And here." His tongue moved down her throat, his lips closing over her skin, his hot, open, wet kisses driving the heat in her body to a critical level.

"Cole..." she tried again. Her knees were weak, her body pliant and soft. She wanted to sink into a puddle on the floor and pull him with her. Lights whirled behind her closed lids. Delight spread as his mouth continued to touch her, caress her, drive her wild with increasing desire. She wanted more.

As if he could read her mind, he picked her up and set her on the edge of the table. Tilting her head back, he continued his assault on her throat, coming time and time again to the rapid pulse point. Then his lips moved lower, following the line of her top, capturing every speck of cream that dotted her flushed skin.

He released her buttons, following the shadow of her breasts.

"Stop." Trisha wished she had more force behind her voice. Intellectually she knew they had to stop, but every cell in her body cried out for more. Threading her fingers into his hair, she held him close to her, telling him to stop, yet belying the command by holding him so he could not.

"Just checking to make sure I get all that cream," he murmured as he trailed his tongue down the slope of one milky white breast. Capturing her nipple, he sucked gently.

The flame seared her. She arched and offered herself to him as she clung to his head, wanting more, so much more. She loved him, had loved him since she'd been a girl of sixteen. Now, after all these years, now he noticed her, touched her, drove her deep into passion as he led her to heights never before dreamed about.

He moved to the other nipple, licking it with soft little laps, pulling it into his hot mouth to lave, love. His hands moved to her thighs, spreading them enough for him to step between them. Then he pulled her against him, settling her body in alignment with his. His shirt was unfastened, and her hot breasts crushed against the strong muscles of his chest as his kisses moved to the sensitive spot behind her ear.

"I told you about your hair," he rasped in her ear as he unfastened it from the topknot that held it off her neck. The soft waves cascaded down, blanketing her, holding in the heat that his touch built.

"It was cooler that way," she whispered, her lips tracing his jaw, her teeth gently nipping his earlobe.

With a growl of masculine domination, he crushed her mouth beneath his, his tongue foraging into her mouth, branding her for all time as his. She pressed in as she returned the fervor of his kiss with deeply buried passion. When his hands skimmed over her hips she thrust forward, settling the heat of her core on top of the strong ridge of his erection. When his fingers came around to slip beneath the edge of her shorts and caress the crease where thigh met hip, she moaned in wondrous delight.

She was going up in smoke and she didn't even care. It was glorious. Heaven was only a moment away. Soon she would share it with Cole.

"Cole? Trisha? Oh, my." Peggy Langford stopped in stunned surprise at the kitchen door.

With a groan of disgust, Cole broke the kiss. He glanced over at his mother, almost yelling out his frustration. Seeing her startled expression, he instead turned back to Trisha and stepped back, bringing the edges of her top together and clumsily fastening a couple of buttons.

"I can do that," she said, her face flaming with embarrassment.

"I'm so sorry. I didn't mean to interrupt," Peggy said.

"It's all right, Mom. I thought we were picking you up at the hospital." Cole gave Trisha another look to make sure she was decent. He wanted to say something, but didn't know the words to ease her embarrassment. He stepped away, allowing her to bring her knees together and hop down from the table. She turned away from him and his mother.

"I got a ride home. I thought I'd change into something that didn't smell like the hospital to go to Becky's. I'm sorry I interrupted." She walked quickly through the kitchen. "Although—" she paused at the door and looked at both of them with a huge grin "—there's nothing wrong in my book with a man showing his love to his wife." With a small laugh, she turned and walked to her room.

Seven

"**T**risha?"

"You better go take your shower. We don't have much time if we want to get to Becky's by six-thirty," she said stiffly, picking up the mixer and switching it on.

Cole's hand covered hers. He flicked off the beaters. "Are you all right?"

"Sure." She kept her gaze on the whipped cream, internally screaming for him to leave before she fell apart.

He cupped her chin and brought her face around, his eyes penetrating. "Embarrassed?"

She nodded. "God, Cole, your *mother!* I can't believe she walked in on us like that. I could just die."

"She didn't seem perturbed. If anything, it reaffirmed her belief in our marriage. Wasn't that the purpose of your kiss a couple days ago?"

"That was different."

"Not as erotic, that's for sure," he teased gently.

She flushed. "Go get dressed and let me finish the cake. We're going to be late."

"So what? We won't be that late, and besides, Becky is family. We'll just tell her—"

"We won't tell her anything. Go!" She glared at him, but he was totally unaffected. Grinning cheekily, he dropped a quick kiss on her lips and turned to saunter from the room as if he had all the time in the world.

Turning back to the cake, Trisha wondered if she could slink off to bed and hide under the covers and never have to face her mother-in-law again. She couldn't believe she had forgotten all sense of decorum. Being in Cole's arms drove every bit of sense from her mind.

Peggy entered the kitchen just as Trisha finished spreading the last of the frosting. She walked over to the younger woman. "I'm sorry I interrupted, Trisha," she began.

"We shouldn't have been doing that here," Trisha said, avoiding the other woman's eyes.

"It did me good to see it, though. I sometimes worried about your marriage. I wondered if Cole treated you like a loved wife. Your wedding seemed like such a rushed affair, just when he got his new job and all. I realize you couldn't wait, but I was worried just the same."

"He's always treated me fine," Trisha said. The last thing she wanted was for Cole's parents to suspect everything wasn't perfect in their world. They didn't need the worry at this stage. Time enough for them to be concerned about their son when Cole went through with the divorce.

"Let me help you get that into the cooler," Peggy offered when Trisha finished.

"Thanks." If her mother-in-law was offering an olive branch, Trisha was willing to take it. It would still be a long time before Trisha would forget her embarrassment, however. "I still need to change. You might want to give Becky a call and tell her we'll be a little late."

Trisha hurried up the stairs and into the bedroom. She paused only a moment when she saw Cole buttoning his shirt. His slacks were still unzipped, awaiting his shirttails. She swallowed hard and brushed past him to go to the closet and pull out a sundress.

"Trish, let's send Mom to Becky's alone and finish what we started downstairs."

She stared down at the white dress with the little blue flowers dotting it. Flicking a glance at Cole, she wished again he'd just once say something she wanted to hear.

"Want me to leave you to dress in private?" he asked.

She nodded, laying the dress across the end of the bed. She would take a quick sponge bath, freshen up just a little before dressing. Give herself time to cool down.

He nodded, his eyes serious. "Okay this time, honey, but not forever."

"What do you mean?"

"I mean we're moving forward in this relationship. It's not going to be like it was in Kuwait." He stopped by the door and looked back at her. "I want you, Trisha. Make no mistake about it. And I know you want me."

That came close to what she wanted to hear. She nodded. There was no use denying the obvious truth. She smiled. "So what are you going to do about it?"

"Tell you later. Or maybe show you later."

Trisha stared at the closed door for a long moment, her imagination flying in fifty different directions. A glance at the clock had her hurrying to get dressed.

Dinner was a joyful affair. With everyone relieved that Matt's prognosis was so favorable, they were able to relax and enjoy the meal. Trevor and Tyler were the center of attention. They were exuberant, outgoing little boys, quick to make friends. After climbing into their grandmother's lap to share special treats with her, they made the rounds.

Cole picked up Trevor when he came over, smiling at his nephew. He was a sturdy boy, easily recognized as Tom's son. He proudly showed Cole his truck and explained how he liked to play with it in the sandbox. Maybe his uncle would go out after dinner and see how it worked, he slyly suggested.

Cole glanced up to see Tyler snuggled up in Trisha's lap, regaling her with stories about a nest of baby birds the boys could see from their window. She leaned over him, totally absorbed in the toddler's tale. Cole's heart jerked as he watched. For the first time in years he thought about a family of his own.

He knew Trisha wanted one. She'd said that was the reason she would look for another husband as soon as their marriage was over. She wanted children, wanted a family to love and belong to. She would be all alone when they separated.

A family. A baby. He'd wanted kids, years ago. Diane had always put off starting a family, saying the time wasn't right. He was glad now that she had. Divorce was hard on kids.

Trisha would be a wonderful mother. He could see her cuddling their own child as she was holding Tyler. *Their own child?* No, he dared not create a baby with her. Not unless they decided to stay married. And that was still up in the air. He knew intellectually that Trisha was nothing like Diane. She didn't gamble. He knew she wasn't seeing anyone on the side. Yet a part of him was still afraid to trust. She'd gone into this marriage for business reasons, just as he had. Would she want to stay married to him? Would she want to start a family with him?

He was almost thirty-two years old. His father had had two kids by the time he was thirty-two. Becky was the same age as Trisha and would have three children in another couple of months. No wonder Trisha didn't want to waste any time finding a mate. Neither one of them was getting younger.

Slowly he turned his attention back to Trevor, but in the back of his mind remained the idea of staying married, starting a family, seeing what life had to offer with Trisha by his side.

After dinner, Becky sent the boys out in the backyard to play while the adults had dessert and coffee.

"I love angel food cake, and the whipped-cream frosting is great," she said as she handed around the plates.

"I'm fond of it, too—wherever I find it," Cole murmured, sitting beside Trisha.

She smiled up at Becky, ignoring Cole, though she tingled in response to the memory his low voice triggered. She finally threw him a glance from beneath her lashes, pleased to find he was studying her.

"And this is for both of you from all of us." Becky handed Trisha a large envelope, with a bright silver bow on top.

"What is it?" Trisha asked, looking at her friend.

Becky grinned and settled awkwardly down beside Tom.

"It's a wedding present. You and Cole married so fast last summer we didn't have time to think up something great. But we have now, and want you to have it."

"We didn't need wedding gifts," Cole said slowly, eyeing the envelope.

"Maybe you didn't, brother dear. It wasn't your first wedding, but it was Trisha's and she deserves something." Becky's glare dared him to argue. Cole nodded and watched as Trisha slowly opened the envelope flap.

"Oh!" She stared at the gift certificate then looked up at Cole, her expression uncertain.

"What is it?"

"A long weekend at the Mar y Sol Hotel at Virginia Beach," she said, naming one of the more exclusive hotels in that resort town.

"Nice." His gaze held hers. He could see her stretched out on the sand, wearing some skimpy bikini. He'd rub oil on her back, down to her hips, along the tops of her thighs. Cole cleared his throat and looked away, before his thoughts betrayed him in front of everyone.

"Thanks, Becky," Trisha said, "Thanks to all of you. This is wonderful."

"Well, no matter what you say, I don't think Kuwait is the ideal honeymoon spot. Now you can take a long weekend, once Dad's better and Cole can break away from work," Becky said brightly. "Or when you hit the *New York Times* bestseller list again."

"*New York Times* bestseller list?" Cole asked.

Trisha's heart sank. She'd never gotten around to telling him. She wished he didn't have to learn about it this way.

Becky stared at her. "Didn't you tell him?"

"Not yet."

"Not yet?" Tom sat up and asked. "The first one was a year ago." He turned to Cole. "Your wife's quite famous. Both her first two books hit the bestseller list within weeks of publication."

"I didn't know," Cole said quietly, his eyes on Trisha. "She didn't mention it." Something cold settled around his heart. Here he'd been thinking about extending the marriage, staying married to Trisha, and she had never even mentioned such a momentous event like her books reaching the *New York Times* list. Obviously she wasn't planning to continue in the marriage. Did she want to end it now that they were back in the States? She had mentioned it, but he had wanted to keep looking after her. Now he wasn't sure what he wanted, what she wanted.

Trisha looked around. Everyone was staring at her, waiting to hear her explanation of why she hadn't related such an important event to her husband. Peggy looked worried and confused, Becky challenging, Tom puzzled. Cole's eyes were narrowed as he gazed impassively at her.

Trisha took a deep breath and turned to Cole. "Actually it was hard to realize over in Kuwait. I mean I just got a note from my agent. And you were so busy, with work and everything. I, uh, I guess it just never seemed the right time to bring it up. You never asked how things were going, so I guess I thought you wouldn't be interested. I'm sorry if I was wrong."

Cole nodded and looked away. What a bastard he'd been. Not once in an entire year had he asked about her writing. He'd made the terms of their marriage, he'd set the pace of their life in Kuwait. No wonder she'd never brought it up—she had ample reason to suspect he wouldn't be interested.

But it made him almost sick to realize something so exciting had happened to her and she'd believed him so disinterested in her life that she wasn't comfortable enough to share it with him. God, he'd thought maybe they could continue being married. He'd never thought that Trisha might not wish to continue.

"How is your current book coming?" Peggy asked, trying to fill the awkward silence.

"I'm doing the last of the revisions."

"Do you have an idea for the next one?" Tom asked.

"I'm playing with some ideas in my head. Once I finish the revisions, I'll try to draw up a proposal for the next one."

"Still using John Taylor as the hero?"

Trisha nodded, glancing at Cole. His expression was set, closed. He stared down at his coffee. Her heart went out to him. She would not have embarrassed him before his family for anything. She should have told him before, whether or not he wanted to hear it. Now it was too late.

When the boys trooped back inside, the atmosphere lightened. Trisha's books were not mentioned again during the evening.

When they were leaving, Cole drew his sister aside. "I assume you have copies of Trisha's books. Can I borrow one to read?"

Becky started to say something, but only nodded and went to fetch the books. Handing all three to Cole, she warned him that she hadn't read the third and he better not crease any of the pages.

"Thanks, Sis. I'll return them when I finish reading them."

"You could have asked Trisha. I know she would have been delighted to have you read her books."

"I should have," was all he said.

Cole bade his mother and Trisha good-night when they reached home, then headed for his father's study, closing the door firmly behind him.

"I guess I blew that, huh?" Trisha said as she heard the door click shut.

"I'm not sure. He could have asked. Isn't that what you were waiting for?" Peggy said.

Trisha nodded her head.

"Sometimes men can be very self-centered. It doesn't mean that they don't love us or care about what we do. They just forget, I guess," Peggy said.

"It's all right, Peggy. Cole had a lot to do in Kuwait. And I should have brought it up. It was stupid to wait for him to ask. Obviously he thought it wasn't important to me because I never talked about my books. I hope he doesn't feel hurt that I didn't tell him."

"You and he need to work this out for yourselves. You don't need nosy in-laws interfering. Good night, my dear. Will you be taking me to the hospital in the morning?"

"Yes. We can be there by nine. I'll visit Matt for a few minutes, then I have to get back to work."

Trisha took a shower before putting on her T-shirt. Once in the large bed, she reached for her notepad. She added sexy nightgown to her growing list. It was time she stopped sleeping in Cole's shirt and found something more alluring. When they left his parents' home, chances were good they would revert to separate bedrooms again. She didn't have much time.

Lying down, she listened to the sounds of the old house settling for the night. Her tenants would be moving out soon and she could move back home. She missed her house. She would be glad to go back home. Would Cole still go with her? Did he still want to stay married? Tonight demonstrated how far apart they really were. Could they bridge the breach and draw closer?

She shook her head to clear it. They needed to talk, and Cole was not a man for talking. Sighing softly, Trisha began to think about a new plot line for her next book. She would finish her line edit by the end of the week. She'd like to come up with at least an idea to pitch to her publisher. Maybe the new story could involve construction. Immediately she saw Cole as he had been the other afternoon—hard hat, tool belt and masculine stance. Taking off the shirt, letting his skin gleam in the sun. Should John Taylor work undercover as a construction worker for this book? She'd never had a permanent love angle. John found a woman in each book to help him, and to offer a fleeting love interest. Was it time to change that?

She sat up and reached for her notebook, jotting down plot points. When finished, she tossed the notebook on the bedside table and switched off the light. She wasn't waiting up for Cole tonight.

Instead she dreamed about the next story idea, mixing construction with underworld crime, Chevy pickups with fancy foreign cars. The blossom of her idea was beginning to unfold.

Cole leaned his head back against the recliner and closed his eyes. He wanted to finish the book tonight but didn't think he'd make it. The words danced before his eyes. Maybe if he rested a bit, he could continue. It was after one.

He needed to get some sleep if he planned to be alert on the job in the morning.

Who would have suspected his shy, innocent, sheltered wife capable of writing such a powerful book? Trisha had never gone anywhere except college in Charlottesville, never done anything except work as a librarian and take care of her father. Yet her writing was strong, clear and captivating. The research he could understand. With her background, she'd know instantly how to locate any fact she needed.

What was so astonishing was the manner in which she was able to draw the reader into the dark underworld of crime and intrigue. The language was gritty and sparse, painting vivid scenes with few words, yet expressing every nuance needed to captivate the reader's attention. He felt as if he were a part of John Taylor's experiences, as if he were right there with the hero.

And the twists and turns of the plot were masterful. How had she known to do all that? And how was she going to let her hero find his way out of the convoluted situation he was in?

This book opened an entirely new dimension to Trisha. Cole wanted to talk to her about her writing, find out why she did it, how she did it. What had first encouraged her to even try to write. And where did she get her ideas?

After he finished this book he'd ask her. He picked it up again, and plunged back into the action.

When Trisha awoke the next morning, the bed beside her was empty. She reached out; the sheets were cool. If Cole had ever come to bed, he'd left hours ago. Sighing softly, she rose and went to get dressed.

When she joined Peggy in the kitchen for breakfast, she asked after Cole.

"He left early. Said there was a lot to do at the site and he wanted to get some time in before going to see his dad. Apparently Matt is questioning him on what's going on and Cole wanted to have all the information available.''

"He and Matt aren't arguing, are they?'' Trisha asked.

"I don't think so. I think Matt just wants to know things are getting back on track. We've talked a bit. I think he's going to give the business up. This heart attack changed the way we think about things. Life is too precious to live with problems we don't need. If Cole wants to run the business, I think Matt's ready to let him.''

"Cole would make changes,'' Trisha warned.

"Matt knows that. He's ready to let go. He wouldn't place any restrictions on Cole if he turns the company over to him. Do you think Cole would take it?''

Trisha nodded. "If he could have total freedom to run it as he wants, I think he would. He might be a bit stubborn about structuring the deal so he doesn't feel Matt is just giving it to him.''

"But why not? Why else does he think Matt built it up except to leave it to Cole?''

"They'll have to work that out by themselves. I just know Cole has a strong streak of independence. He doesn't like depending on anyone, or feeling as if he's been given a handout.''

"Then let's hope Matt knows that, as well.''

When they arrived at the hospital, Matt was much improved. Many of the tubes and wires had been removed. Only the IV and one cardiac monitor remained. He was sitting up in bed and looked almost healthy. Trisha was glad for the improvement. It meant more to see him this way than to hear the doctor say he would recover. She visited for a few minutes, then gave him a quick kiss on the cheek, saying she'd see him later. She knew he and Peggy wanted to be together.

Revisions went a little easier. But instead of fantasizing about Cole and his kisses, Trisha found herself worrying from time to time about his reaction to the fact she hadn't told him about her books. He'd not said a word, and that concerned her. Was he furious, or hurt? Had he started to read one of her books last night? She'd seen the stack Becky had given him. He could have asked her; she had her author's copies just collecting dust in their boxes.

Had he come to bed at all last night, or was he already pulling away?

She couldn't stand the uncertainty. Dialing the construction site, Trisha waited impatiently for someone to answer.

"Langford Construction," Cole said sharply.

"Have you had lunch yet?" she asked.

"Trisha? No, I haven't eaten."

"I could bring you something."

The silence stretched endlessly before he replied. "I'd like that. Bring it around one. I'll take a break then."

She hung up almost giddy with relief. Saving her work, she went to the kitchen to see what kind of sumptuous lunch she could make.

When she arrived, he was working on the joists of one of the houses. Leaving the basket of food in the cool office, she went searching for him. Spotting him on the high beams, Trisha was content to watch him work. He had discarded his shirt and his skin gleamed in the hot sun. His tan was even and dark. She remembered glimpsing the lighter skin below his waist when he'd opened the bathroom door the other evening. She swallowed hard with the memory.

He saw her and waved. Finishing the job he was doing, he called something to the others working on the framing and climbed down the ladder.

"Lunch?" he asked, drawing near.

She nodded, letting her eyes boldly roam over his chest, down the long legs encased in snug jeans. Raising her gaze to meet with his, she let her appreciation show. He smiled and reached out to capture the nape of her neck in his hard hand, drawing her up for his kiss.

He smelled of fresh cut wood and sunshine and male sweat. Trisha drew in a deep breath, opening her mouth to his, reveling in the heady sensations his touch always brought.

"So what's for lunch?" he said, setting her back and turning toward the trailer. He shrugged into a shirt, then his hand drifted down to clasp with hers as they walked carefully across the construction site.

"Fried chicken, hot biscuits, iced tea and an orange."

"No cake?"

"We left it with Becky."

"Umm, wouldn't mind some of that whipped cream, never mind the cake." He held the door open for her, his expression teasing.

Trisha relaxed. It was going to be all right. He wasn't mad, didn't seem hurt. He was the teasing man she so often found.

When they had made a makeshift table from the second desk and began to eat, Cole said, "I read one of your books last night, *Open the Gate to Death*."

"And?"

"I see why it hit the bestseller list. You've got a tremendous talent, honey."

"So you liked it?"

"I sure did. I have two more to read."

"You don't have to do that, you know." She didn't want him to feel obligated to read her books.

"I want to read them. Then I'm going to cross-examine you like John Taylor does to the perps. How did you ever get into writing stories like this?"

She smiled and shrugged. "They just come to me. Although, I have to do tons of research. Especially for the first one—I didn't have a clue about guns and other weapons. But it filled the nights." She snapped her mouth shut before she gave away the true reason she'd started writing. She'd never expected to marry, rarely dated and found the outlet of writing enough to give her a measure of contentment she hadn't expected.

"I've got another way to fill your nights, now," he said.

She blinked. "What?"

Reaching out, he cupped her chin, tracing his thumb across her lower lip, tugging a little, brushing back and forth. "Tonight, you and I are going to excuse ourselves early and go to bed. And we are *not* going to sleep."

"We're not?" Her heart pounded in her chest, the blood surged through her veins.

Slowly he shook his head, his eyes looking deep into hers, desire clearly showing.

She gripped his wrist, holding on for dear life, lest she float away. "What time are you coming home?" she asked softly.

"I'll be home by six. We'll eat, call to see how Dad's doing and go to bed."

Trisha licked suddenly dry lips, touching her tongue against his thumb, tasting him, anticipation building sweet and strong. She wanted the afternoon to pass swiftly and night to fall fast. She wanted to savor the promise in his eyes, relish the growing excitement that swelled deep inside her. She felt the rising tension as the image of his words burned into her mind. She wanted the day to end—now.

"So are you writing this afternoon?" he asked.

"If I can concentrate," she said, pulling away. "You didn't make that easy with your comment."

He chuckled and leaned back, watching her closely.

"Good. I've been thinking about you since we woke up yesterday morning. Time enough now to end this suspense."

"Sex games," she murmured.

"Hot and sensational."

"I don't have much practice."

"We can practice together."

Trisha took a deep breath. "I need to get back home."
Lunch was over. The afternoon would prove endless, but the
sooner she got out of his way, the sooner he'd finish for the
day and come home. Besides, she wanted to do some shopping. Time to use some of the items on her list.

And moving up to the top of the list was a new nightgown. Something very feminine, very different from a util-
itarian T-shirt.

By the time Trisha finished shopping and returned home
it was time to start dinner. There was a message on the answering machine from Peggy saying she wouldn't be home
until late. Friends had joined her at the hospital and wanted
to take her to dinner when she left for the day.

Trisha played the message through a second time, her
heart pounding with the implications. She and Cole would
not have to wait until bedtime. Peggy wouldn't be home.
The house would be theirs all evening.

Trying to ignore the pull of excitement that swept through
her, Trisha continued up the stairs to unpack her new
clothes. She drew out the sexy nightie. It was pale peach,
short, with lots of lace and ribbons. She felt like a new
bride. Which she was, if truth be known. This would be her
wedding night.

Spreading it out on the bed, she then pulled out the new
shorts and top she hadn't been able to resist. She swiftly
changed. The shorts were short, exposing the entire length
of her thigh. The top was cropped, ending above her waist-
band, exposing an inch or so of abdomen. It buttoned in the
front like the top she'd worn to whip the cream. Would Cole
wish to unfasten these buttons?

Brushing out her hair, she deliberately fastened it on top
of her head again, letting wispy tendrils float down around

her face. She glanced in the mirror, satisfied with the effect.

If he wanted to play sex games, she was willing to accommodate him. And maybe teach him something in the process.

Eight

Trisha decided to make a salad for dinner. That would be quick and easy, and not involve cooking. Since just the two of them would be home for dinner, they could eat in the backyard. She hoped that would prove more comfortable than eating in the warm kitchen. She prepared a large garden salad, then sliced cold ham and turkey and cheese onto it. Whipping up a batch of corn bread, she plopped it into the oven just as Cole arrived home.

"Dinner will be ready soon," she said as he walked into the kitchen, feeling a sudden attack of shyness hit her.

He eyed her up and down, his eyes gleaming at the sight of her shorts, the cropped top. Smiling in a satisfied way, he strode quickly across the room. Tipping up her chin, he brushed his lips across hers. "Why wait for dinner? You look good enough to eat right now."

She pushed gently against his shoulder, warmth from his words matching the heat from the oven.

"Go take your shower, but make it quick. The corn bread will be ready in about fifteen minutes."

He was back in ten.

"Your mother is eating out with friends tonight," Trisha told him when he rejoined her. "Would you like beer or iced tea to drink?"

"Tea. When is she coming home?" Cole leaned against the doorjamb, watching Trisha move around the kitchen. Wearing cutoff jeans and a short-sleeved, cotton shirt left unbuttoned, he was as cool as he was going to get this evening. And watching his sexy little wife was raising his temperature. His eyes were drawn to the smooth expanse of legs revealed by her shorts. The way the cotton clung to the gentle swell of her hips and bottom made his hand itch to touch her. He wasn't sure he wanted dinner. He was sure he wanted Trisha.

"Late. I hope she can enjoy herself."

"Huh?" He'd missed part of what she'd said, thinking of getting her in bed, of peeling off that skimpy little top, slipping her out of those indecently short shorts and kissing every inch of her delectable body.

Trisha eyed him suspiciously. "I said your mother would be late getting home."

"Good." He pushed away from the door and walked over to her, reaching out to draw her into his arms.

The afternoon was hot, but the heat from Cole was scorching. Trisha opened her mouth under his and pressed eagerly against him, feeling the hard, sleek muscles of his chest. Only the soft cotton of her top separated them. The potency of his kiss curled her toes.

Beneath his talented mouth, the kitchen faded from her consciousness. His kiss carried her to a magical place of sexual sensations and pleasure. His tongue tasted her, inflamed her, captivated her, as she spiraled to heightened awareness. He brought forth the secret yearnings and cravings that had been buried deep within her. His special touch awoke her to enchantments never before known.

She wanted more. Her lips moved against his, her tongue daringly invaded his mouth, learning him, mating with his, luring him back to her.

His hands slipped beneath her top, spanned her waist, his thumbs making wicked circles against her belly, dipping in the slight hollow of her navel, skimming her hipbones. She moved against him, rubbing her breasts against his chest like a sensuous cat, longing for his touch there, longing for his hands to roam over her.

Slowly one hand rode up, encountered her bare breast and paused. Trisha trembled with suspense. She held her breath, her whole being focused on Cole's hand. Her whole being longed to know the pleasure only he could bring. When he cupped her, she sighed and leaned against him, pressing herself into him, wanting more. More.

Lazily he caressed her, his thumb slowly stroking over her, bringing her to quivering awareness, throbbing attention. She traced his neck, the powerful muscles in his shoulders. Slowly she trailed her fingers down his chest, flicking one against a flat nipple, smiling inside at his sudden in-drawn breath.

When his mouth moved to kiss her cheek, nip lightly at her ear, trail kisses down her neck, she arched back to give him complete access. She continued to rub against him, moving her own hands across his body, learning him as he learned her.

The steady ding-ding of the oven timer finally penetrated, pushed back the sensual haze. Slowly she pulled back.

"Cole, I have to get the corn bread. It'll burn otherwise."

"Umm. Let it." His mouth captured hers again.

She kissed him briefly, the pulled back. "Stop. Let me just get the corn bread out."

Pulling away, Trisha spun around to silence the annoying timer. Pulling open the oven door, she was enveloped by the heat. It still didn't compare to her own temperature when Cole was kissing her.

Lifting out the pan, she set it on the counter.

"Don't you want dinner?" she asked. "I made a big salad and thought we could eat outside."

Cole looked once more at her mouth, as if he would forget dinner and take her in his arms again. But he shrugged. "Sure, sounds good."

Working together, they soon had the meal on the old picnic table beneath the large oak behind the house. Conversation was easy between them as they enjoyed the pleasant coolness in the yard. The old oak trees offered shelter from the heat of the waning afternoon sun. The high hedges on both sides offered total privacy from the neighbors. In the back, the yard sloped down to a small wooded area. As the sun sank in the west, twilight cloaked them in a warm intimate world of two.

The evening reminded Trisha of some of the better memories she had of Kuwait. The ones where Cole had come home for dinner and stayed to talk to her rather than returning to work, or going to bed early. Such evenings had been rare and she had cherished them all the more when they'd come.

They discussed his dad's prognosis and how soon he might be released from the hospital. Cole spoke of the work going on at the Windmere site and related some of the problems facing Langford Construction. Trisha mentioned talking to the real estate agent about how soon her tenants might be expected to move out.

When they finished eating, they moved to the wooden swing. Trisha wondered if Cole was as reluctant to end the pleasant moment as she was.

"Tired?" she asked sympathetically.

"Yeah." He leaned his head back and closed his eyes. Strain and tension were evident in the lines beside his mouth, in the tense way he held himself.

Trisha's heart ached as she sat beside him and sipped her iced tea. He gently pushed them back and forth in the swing. The silence was comfortable between them. The night was still and hot; the sun's setting had not cooled things off appreciably. She gazed out over the colorful garden, enjoying the serenity and peace. It reminded her of her own yard. She wondered how her flowers had fared with her tenants. She hoped they had survived; she loved the various beds she'd planted in past years.

Trisha sat quietly in the swing, growing more and more conscious of Cole sitting only inches away. She couldn't think of anything else to say. She could see his large capable hands holding his glass, raising it to his lips from time to time to sip. The same lips that had her mindless with sensations whenever they touched her. His legs were stretched out, moving just a little as he pushed the swing to and fro. His shirt had fallen open, his chest showing a deep tan against the soft blue of the shirt. His nipples showed even darker.

She licked her lips and tried to move her gaze. Tightening her hold on the cold glass, she resisted the urge to brush her fingertips across those flat male nipples, resisted the need in her to take up where they had stopped in the kitchen. Was he waiting for some sign from her that she wanted him to continue where they'd left off?

Cole looked over at her from beneath half-closed lids. He reached out and took her glass from her fingers and set both their glasses on the grass beneath the swing. Trisha brushed her hands against her shorts to still their nervous energy.

"Come here," he said.

She hesitated only a moment. Then, taking a deep breath, she slowly moved, surprising Cole by daring to slip across his legs, straddling him, sitting on his thighs facing him, her knees on either side of his hips, her bottom sinking down on the tops of his thighs. Tilting her head, she studied him in the waning light, hoping he couldn't feel her rapid heartbeat. It was twilight, the soft time of day when things blurred as the light faded from the sky. Soon it would be dark. But for now there was plenty of soft seductive light to see by.

"Well?" he asked, a lopsided smile on his face as his eyes gazed into hers. His hands caressed her legs, his thumbs slipping beneath the edges of her shorts, caressing the soft, silky skin he found.

"Well." She took a deep breath, wondering if she could go through with it. All day she'd been on tenterhooks of anticipation. He'd said they would make love tonight. She wanted it as much as he did, maybe more. Slowly, her eyes never leaving his, her right hand came up to the top button of her shirt. She slid it through the hole.

Cole guessed her intent. His smile faded as he watched her. His gaze flicked to the top of her shirt, back to her eyes.

The hunger Trisha saw reflected there excited her. Slowly, Trisha's hand slid down to the next button, and slid it through its hole. The shirt opened slightly in a small V at the top.

She undid two more buttons, never taking her eyes from his. Her fingers trembled slightly. She hoped she wasn't making a fool of herself. But she wanted this too much to stop. Now the dark shadow of her cleavage began to show as the cropped top opened in a wider V, peeling down as it was released from the fasteners.

Cole's hands stopped, gripping her thighs as he watched Trisha unfasten yet another button. His eyes gleamed in the twilight. Slowly her hand moved to the next one.

He could see the gentle swells of her breasts now in the opening, the soft light blurring their shape slightly. He could feel the heat emanating from her, on his legs, his hips, even through the air between their bodies. He longed to rip the rest of the top open and pull her against him to feel her skin against his. But he clamped down on his desire, savoring the sexy little moves his wife was making for him.

Trisha felt him grow harder beneath her and she smiled, her eyes still watching him watch her. Her heart filled with love, spilled it through her body. She so wanted to make love with him, just one time. To show him what she could not say. To love him.

Another button.

"Trisha."

"Your top's open, shouldn't mine be?" she said softly, as yet another button slid from its hole.

"You're driving me crazy, Trish," Cole said hoarsely.

She smiled at his tone and her hand slid to the next button. Her left hand reached out to push his shirt a bit off his shoulder, trace her fingertips down his chest, lightly brushing against his nipple. His hands tightened. Trisha undid another button. Only two more remained.

Her shirt gaped open, caught on the tips of her breasts, displaying the full valley between, the soft slopes, the muscles of her stomach.

When she reached the last button, she paused. Cole groaned. Smiling in triumph, she slid it free.

He pulled her hips higher, settling her on his lap, then slowly moved his hands to the edges of her shirt, his eyes holding hers, deep and mysterious.

She arched her back a little and waited for his move.

Slowly his hands spread her shirt. He watched as the edges moved apart, caught on her nipples, then snapped free. He left her shirt on her shoulders, hanging down to frame her breasts. Slowly his hands covered her stomach, his fingers tracing fire and ice as he caressed the satiny skin.

Trisha trembled, her heart slamming against her chest, waiting endlessly for the contact that would send her over the edge.

He smiled a little and traced the soft skin beneath her breasts, skimming lightly over her to the sides, drawing a finger down the valley between.

She moved restlessly, shifting her weight on her bottom, feeling the hard arousal he didn't even try to hide.

"Don't be mean, Cole," she said softly, wanting his hands to touch her where she ached most, to fondle her and caress her and love her. Trisha was almost overwhelmed with the throbbing desire that centered deep inside her. Longing for him to caress her until she was mindless with delight and pleasure, she moved against his hands, offering him all the love within her.

"What is it you want, Trisha?" he said softly, his fingers skimming just beneath her nipples.

"You know. Touch me where I want you to," she said, clenching her teeth against the longing, her hands stroking the hard muscles of his chest.

"Here, maybe?" he said, with a feather-light touch to one nipple.

She moaned softly. She was going to die craving his touch. And he was mean to tease her so.

"Maybe here?" he said, pulling her down against him and capturing one rosy tip in his hot mouth. His tongue was hard, his caress exciting, electrifying. Trisha felt the exhilarating pull deep within her and she captured his head in her hands, threading her fingers in the thick mane of hair, holding him tightly against her, not wanting him to ever leave.

Her hips rocked against his as Cole kissed her and suckled her breast, laving the nipple, nipping it gently, soothing it. When he pulled away, she almost cried, but it was only to allow him to capture the other nipple.

With a sigh of relief, she gave herself over to the rapture Cole brought. Her fingers moved against his shoulders, feeling his hot skin, pushing frantically at his shirt to get it off so there was nothing between them. There was only his skin and hers, only Cole and her.

He sat up and peeled off his shirt, tossing it aside. Slowly he eased them off the swing, down to the cool grass, Trisha still in his lap.

Turning her, he laid her on their shirts and followed to lie over her, still between her thighs, his chest pressing against her breasts. She looked up at him briefly before his mouth reclaimed hers and she was lost.

It was like riding a Ferris wheel, or a magic carpet, like seeing fireworks or northern lights, like being loved and desired and cherished. She was pleasured all through her body. Her hands touched his back, her breasts were pressed to his chest, her legs tangled with his.

The soft twilight was gone and only the hot dark night surrounded them, enclosed them. Heat spiraled up through her as she writhed gently in increasing delight at the intensity of emotions building. She was intoxicated with the sensuous sensations Cole's touch induced, soaring beyond the realms of reality to the rapture that beckoned.

"Trisha." Cole's mouth was still against hers, his lips moving against hers as he spoke. "Trisha, I want you. Now."

She rocked her hips against his, her hands kneading the muscles of his back.

"Yes."

He pulled back a few inches so he could see her. It had grown dark, quiet, still. She barely discerned his head silhouetted against the slight light spilling out from the kitchen. Her heart pounded and she drew in ragged gulps of air to cool her heated body. They were concealed in darkness—the soft warm darkness of the Southern night, the soft warm darkness of love.

Cole reached for her hands, pulled them over her head and held them there with his. His weight was heavy on her breasts and she looked up at him. What would happen next?

She was burning up with love for him. She was panting, her lips swollen and achy. She ached for his touch, his inflaming kisses.

"I thought we would do this in bed," Cole said as his hands released the fastenings on her shorts and began to work them down her hips.

"Too far away," Trisha said, threading her fingers through his, watching as he tugged open his cutoffs.

In only seconds both were naked in the sultry night. Cole gently nudged her legs apart and settled himself between them. Trisha pulled her hands free and moved them across his damp body, urging him closer, her legs coming around his waist. He cupped her face with his palms, his mouth moving over hers as he plunged into the heat that awaited him.

He wasn't gentle or slow. In only seconds they were straining against each other. He pressed deep within her, setting the pace fast and furious. She rose to meet each thrust. The heat was incredible; she was burning up. He moved with her, driving her higher and higher, hotter and hotter. When the clenching heat peaked, Trisha drew her mouth from his to draw in gulps of air. Nothing could cool her; she was on fire for him.

Cole opened his hot mouth on her throat, moved to her shoulders, nipping lightly as the tension between them shimmered even higher. She was going to flash into flame. The dizzying heights, the searing heat, all combined to explode into the sweetest passion she'd ever known. When the final flame erupted, it centered in her womb, spreading out in concentric circles to her fingers and toes, to the end of time. She was mindless with pleasure, with pure exquisite delight.

The waves continued endlessly. Over and over her body convulsed with his, her hands clutching for a hold onto life. Her mouth needed to connect with his. She had never felt so much a part of another person. She knew she would never feel this way with anyone else.

Slowly, slowly, she began to come back to earth. Gasping for breath, she began to grow cognizant of her surroundings. The grass beneath her was crushed, its fragrance permeating the heat surrounding them. The ground was hard, Cole's weight pressed her down.

She began to relax, tracing lazy circles on his muscular back, relishing the feel of his sweat-soaked muscles beneath her fingertips. Her own body was wet, hot, sated. Slowly Trisha felt tears of joy fill her eyes, spill over. It had been the most glorious experience of her life. She gulped back a sob.

"Trish?" Cole rose up on his elbows and tried to see her. "Did I hurt you?" His thumb brushed across her cheek, wiping away a trail of tears. "Honey, did I hurt you?"

She shook her head, afraid to trust her voice.

"Then why the tears?" His voice was concerned.

"Too many emotions, I guess," she whispered.

He brushed his mouth against hers, never wanting to move. It had been incredible. Even better than anything he'd felt with Diane in the first heady months of their marriage. He felt connected to Trisha in a way he had never felt connected to anyone else.

Settling his chin against her shoulder, he breathed deeply. Mixed with grass and love and the roses his mother raised was Trisha's own sweet scent. Lightly he kissed her shoulder where he'd bitten her. It was impossible, but he wanted her again. Now.

Trisha kissed his neck, moved one hand up to play with his hair. She smiled, tears under control. "That was nice. We should have played sex games before," she said softly.

Cole stiffened. Pulling back, he tried to see her expression in the dark. For some reason he didn't like her calling their lovemaking sex games. It had meant more. He wasn't just playing.

Yet, what was he doing?

He withdrew and rolled over on his back, the question echoing again and again. What was he doing with Trisha? Did he want to try for a future together? Could they make their marriage work? He certainly didn't have to worry at all about compatibility in bed. She was dynamite. She'd been giving out signals for days now and he couldn't believe it had taken him so long to respond. Now that they had made love once, he wanted her again. And he suspected he'd want her for a long time to come.

"Oh, God." Cole closed his eyes. How could he have been so carried away?

"What?"

"Trisha, I didn't use anything for birth control," he said, rising up on his elbow to try to see her again.

She turned on her side, away from him, her knees drawn up against her chest. "It's okay," she said softly.

"You're on something?" he asked for clarification.

She shook her head. "No, but it's okay."

"Wrong time of the month?"

She rolled onto her back, turning her head to gaze at him. Cole reached out and rested his hand on her belly, as if needing some connection between them.

"It's too late to worry about anything, but I think I'm safe." For one glorious moment she wondered what it would be like to be pregnant with Cole's baby. She would love to be the mother of his child, of his children. He would make such a wonderful father.

"It would complicate the hell out of our arrangement if you became pregnant," he said. For a moment he felt a flash of panic. He didn't want to be trapped into marriage with anyone. Then he shook his head. Here he had been contemplating staying married to Trisha and now he was worried he might have to do so? He was going crazy. And she was the reason. He couldn't think around her. Later, when he was alone, he'd think it all through.

"Want to go upstairs?" he asked, rubbing her soft skin.

"Yes." She sat up and felt around for her clothes. "We probably should get inside before your mother returns home. I don't want to traipse through her house with grass in my hair and stained and wrinkled clothes. How would we explain that?"

He chuckled, standing, then reached down to haul her to her feet. "If we're real lucky, we can make a dash for it now and not bother to get dressed."

She giggled softly, the adventure of the evening like wine through her veins. She picked up everything—shorts, panties, top. "I'm game if you are. I get the shower first." Trisha turned and walked swiftly toward the gleaming light of the kitchen.

Cole stopped her when they were inside, pulling her clothes from the bunched-up pile she held before her and holding out one of her arms. His hot glance seared its way down her body.

"You are beautiful, Trish," he said, meeting her gaze. Dropping a quick kiss on her mouth, he nodded that she should precede him through the house.

When Trisha gained the safety of the bathroom, she sighed. It had been wonderful! Would he make love to her again when they were in bed? She ran the shower and stepped beneath the warm water. Before she could reach for the soap, however, Cole pushed back the curtain and stepped inside.

"Cole, what are you doing?"

"Saving Mom some water. Want me to wash your back?"

Trisha bit her lip, then nodded and handed him the soap. This was more than she had ever expected. She would hold on to it with both hands.

Cole soaped her body slowly, letting his hands and eyes explore every inch of her. She was so pretty. How had he known her for so many years and not realized it? Her breasts were full and firm, the tips rosy and tempting. Her waist was narrow and her hips flared gently. Over and over he stroked his slippery hands over the swell of her bottom, pulling her up against him, rubbing his own water-slicked skin against hers.

She blushed once or twice, which charmed him more than anything he'd known. She'd made love before, had made love with him just a short time ago, yet she seemed as shy and innocent as a young girl.

When the water began to run cold, he turned it off and helped her out of the shower. Drying them both, he opened the door and listened for any sounds of his mother's return. Apparently she was still visiting with her friends or had gone back to the hospital. He turned and picked Trisha up, cradling her against his chest.

"Cole!"

"Yes?"

"I can walk."

"Indulge me." He closed their bedroom door behind them and laid her on the bed. Coming down on top of her before she could move, he skimmed his hands across her shoulders, her arms, her breasts and down to the top of her thighs. His eyes devoured her as his hands continued their exploration.

Her expression changed to hunger. Her hands tentatively moved over his body, and he felt himself growing even harder. He wanted her. He had wanted her in Kuwait, but she had never given any indication she would be interested. He had wanted her since he woke up with her in his arms the first morning they'd been back home. He wanted her every time he looked at her. And for the time they remained together, he would have her. She had been willing at last and he would use that willingness to satisfy them both.

When she was ready, he again sheathed himself in the honey-hot heat that beckoned. Taking his time, he slowed his pace, endeavoring to make the sensations last forever. Softly he stroked her, his fingers already moving in remembered rhythm to her pleasure. He tasted her with his mouth, his tongue caressing hers, moving to test her skin. He held off moving, lying between her legs, drawing every bit of anticipation to feed their hunger. He wanted them both to savor the exquisite feelings that were building.

Only when she cried out his name and bucked beneath him, urging him to finish, did he allow himself to set a tempo that brought them higher and higher until they crested the summit together and plunged down the other side.

Even before his breathing was steady again he knew she'd fallen asleep. Lying sprawled beneath him like a boneless rag doll, her breathing was deep and even. Her hands fell limply from his back.

Cole kissed her gently on her mouth and rolled to his side, gathering her up to sleep in his arms.

Nine

Trisha awoke the next morning knowing something was different. For a long moment she lay cocooned in the warmth of Cole's arms, wondering what it was. Then she remembered. Opening her eyes, she turned her head until she could see him. He was still sleeping, one arm across her as if holding her against escape. The sheet was kicked away and they lay only in the warmth of the early-morning sun.

Last night had been the most wonderful experience of her life. She smiled slightly in remembrance. He'd been a fantastic lover. Only...

Only there had been no words of love. None from him. None from her. She was afraid to say anything unless he spoke first. The painful memories of her teenage years surfaced. She couldn't forget how he'd laughed with those other boys when discussing the crush she'd had. Only it had been love. Even then, she'd known she loved Cole Langford.

Had anything changed because of last night? Or was Cole taking advantage of what she so freely offered? He'd mentioned sex games—was that all it was to him? For her it had been a joining of her soul to his. Was it only a joining of two bodies to him?

She'd said she would be satisfied with a night. But now she knew that would never be enough. In fact, a lifetime with Cole might not be enough. Had last night changed anything for him, or was he still planning to end their temporary marriage once his father recovered?

She slipped from the bed, careful not to awaken him. The future was too nebulous to consider right now. She would draw on the patience that she'd learned when her father had been so ill, and wait and see.

"Good morning, Peggy. How was your dinner out?" Trisha greeted her mother-in-law when she walked into the kitchen a short time later, dressed for the hospital.

"Hi, honey. It was quite nice. Marjorie and Edith stopped by the hospital and spent a few minutes with Matt. Then we went to that new fish place down on Granby. Goodness, we got to talking and catching up on all the news until it was after eleven when we left. I've been so tied up with Matt I've let my friends slide."

"I'm sure they understand. It looks as if it did you good to go out for once." Trisha smiled, noting the animation in Peggy's face.

"I'm starting to feel more normal. Each day that passes lets me believe just a little more that the doctor knows what he's talking about when he says Matt will be fine."

"Oh, Peggy, I'm sure the doctor wouldn't have said it if he didn't mean it." Once again Trisha imagined how she would feel if it had been Cole so dangerously near death. She would have been afraid, too.

"I know, but it was so hard, almost losing Matt like that. I think I'll live with that fear for a long time."

"Live with what a long time?" Cole stepped into the kitchen. He gave his mother a quick kiss on her cheek, then turned to Trisha. Drawing her into his arms as if he'd done it all his life, he kissed her hard, opening her lips for a brief foray of his tongue before setting her back.

Heat and color high in her cheeks, she stared at him in startled surprise.

"Good morning." His voice was low and husky, sending tantalizing waves of hunger along her nerves.

"Hi."

"I was saying I would have to live with the fear of your father dying for a long time," his mother said, pouring him a cup of coffee. "Here, take this to the table. I'll have breakfast ready in a jiffy."

"You don't have to cook breakfast. I can do that," Trisha protested.

"I'd like to. Then I want to go to the hospital." Peggy glanced over from the stove. "You two sure went to bed early last night. The house was dark when I got home."

Cole shrugged. "Still adjusting to this time zone, I guess." He winked at Trisha.

She dropped her gaze to her coffee, wishing that they had been alone. She should have waited for him to wake up. Maybe then she could have gotten some answers to the questions dancing around in her head. But she would not voice them now. For the time being, she'd be patient.

When Trisha and Peggy arrived at the hospital, they found Matt sitting up in bed, excited to be moving to the regular medical wing that morning. "No more intensive cardiac care needed," he said proudly. "The doctor says I'm recovering in record time. Maybe I can even be discharged later this week."

"Oh, that would be so wonderful!" Peggy exclaimed.

Trisha added her agreement, but wondered what it would do to her relationship with Cole. Was Matt recovered enough to learn his son and his wife were separating? Or would he still need to be sheltered from such news for a while longer?

"Cole coming to see me tonight?" he asked.

"Yes. After work," Trisha replied.

"It's so good to see you both. I'm glad you're back home where you belong. Didn't know I'd have to go to such lengths to get the two of you back, though."

She grinned at his joking. "We're glad to be back. I'm sorry you went to such lengths, too."

Matt reached for his wife's hand, held it in his as he looked shrewdly at Trisha. "I'm going to turn over Langford Construction to Cole. I'm retiring. This scare showed me how much I cherish life. From now on I'm going to do my best to enjoy whatever time I have left. I built up that business for him. Now I'm giving it to him."

Trisha nodded, not knowing what to say. "What will you do?"

Smiling up at Peggy, he answered, "Take a cruise for a start. Something we've talked about for years. Never managed it. We never had many vacations. I was too caught up in the company." He leveled a glare at Trisha. "Don't let Cole make the same mistakes. He needs to take vacations and delegate work. I should have learned that long ago."

"At least it's not too late now, Matt," Peggy said.

"We've been lucky," he said.

Feeling decidedly de trop, Trisha said goodbye and headed back for the house. She had lots of work to do. She'd been mooning around Cole Langford long enough. Time to get to work.

Cole stopped after work to visit his father.

"Didn't know you had moved," he said when he entered his father's semiprivate room. The second bed was empty. Drawing up a chair, Cole sprawled in it, his long legs stretched out before him. No need to tell his father that when he'd gone to the other room and found the bed empty he'd thought the worst for a second. He'd need his dad around for a long time.

"Glad you came by, son. Got something to tell you. I'm signing over Langford Construction. As of today, it's yours."

Cole sat up at that, staring at his father.

"You can't do that, Dad. It's your company. You've built it up from nothing to a very successful venture."

"Which has been waning lately. I haven't had the energy to keep it up."

"That was because of your illness. Now that you're on the mend, you'll bounce back full of energy."

Matt shook his head. "No more interest. I built up the company for you and Becky. It was always to be for you two. I'm signing it over to you now while you're young enough to make a difference with it. Some of the shares will go to your sister, and I'll still want some income from it. But it's yours. You can put up your custom houses if that's what you want, or continue in the development business as I did."

Cole was stunned. "I don't know, Dad—"

"Nothing to know. It's done, as soon as the attorney gets the papers for me to sign. It'll be yours—you can do whatever you want. Sell it if you don't want it." Matt leaned back, studying his son.

"Of course I'd never sell it! I don't know what to say."

"Just say you'll make it the best dang construction company in the Tidewater."

"You mean, keep it the best in the Tidewater."

"Thanks, son. Did you hear that if I continue to improve as rapidly as I've done so far I'll be coming home at the end of the week?"

"That's great, Dad."

Cole paused at the top of the hospital steps, his thoughts miles away. With Trisha, to be precise. Slowly walking toward the pickup truck, he wondered what his father's coming home would mean. It wouldn't be long before his father and mother would no longer need to be sheltered from anything. And by then, Cole had to make up his mind what he wanted. Dared he risk staying married? *"I find I like being part of a couple."* Trisha's words echoed in his mind. Hell, he liked being part of a couple, too, with Trisha the other part. And there was nothing saying he had to make a decision today. They had plenty of time. It would be weeks before his father was totally recovered. Time enough then to decide.

Trisha was still at her computer when he arrived home. Swinging by the dining room, he watched her for a long moment before she knew he was there.

"Oh, hi. I didn't hear you." She caught a glimpse of him from the corner of her eye and smiled up at him.

Cole's gaze fastened on her mouth. Crossing the room in three long steps, he pulled her chair out and leaned over to kiss her, one hand against her head, holding her close.

"Writing going okay?" he asked.

"Yes. Today was very productive. How did things go at the site?"

"They're improving. Where's Mom?"

"She's at Becky's. She'll be home for dinner. I have a ham in the oven. You're home early."

"I went by to see Dad, then just came on home. I need to shower. Come up with me." He reached for her hand, lacing his fingers with hers.

"All right." She pressed the Save button and rose.

He wanted to tell her about his dad's decision, but something held him back, a certain lack of trust. He remembered Diane and how he had once thought he could trust her. He couldn't risk it again.

Maybe he couldn't trust Trisha, but he wanted her.

"Now we have a problem," he said as he led her into their bedroom and closed the door behind him.

"We do?" She turned to face him, a shimmer of fear starting, until she saw the teasing lights in his eyes. She relaxed and tilted her head as she waited for what he had to say.

"I've been working all day and know I'm dirty and sweaty and need a shower. But after we do what I want to do, we're both going to be sweaty and need a shower. So do we shower first, then again, or just wait?"

She stepped into his arms, her own encircling his neck as she leaned against him, drawing his head down for a kiss.

"As I see it, your clothes are what are dirty, so if you take them off, that solves that problem. As to the rest, in the interest of conserving water, which you so rightly pointed out last night was our duty, we should only shower once."

"Your logic, as always, is unassailable." He scooped her up and carried her to bed.

Their clothes were discarded in record time. Cole switched on the window air conditioner. "You generate enough heat, honey," he said, coming back to the bed.

He felt a sense of rightness when he reached for Trisha, a sense of celebration. Maybe he hesitated to tell her of his father's decision, but he could express his deep satisfaction with her in bed. Her soft murmurs inflamed him, her hands moving over his skin excited him as no other ever had. Her mouth welcomed his, and her body joined his in perfect harmony. Time lost meaning, stood still, sped by. It didn't matter. They were in a world of their own, one of tactile sensations, whispered words and pulse-pounding need.

He paused only once to find a small foil packet and don the contents.

Trisha looked at him, puzzled.

"No need to keep taking chances," he whispered against her breast as he moved over her.

She was hot and she was sweet and it was obvious she wanted him with an equal fervor. He would never get enough of this woman, he thought as they exploded together in a searing climax.

Trisha knew she had to open her eyes, but she was floating on a cloud of bliss. She never wanted to have to move, never wanted to resume life as she knew it. If she could float on the sensations Cole brought her, she'd be content the rest of her life.

"You okay?" his voice mumbled gentle in her ear.

She smiled and nodded, her arms still encircling him, her legs still tangled with his. Soon they would have to move, have to shower and go down for dinner when his mother returned home. But not yet. For the moment she wanted to just float.

When he rolled off her, the cool air from the window air conditioner chilled her skin. She curled up into a ball, wishing he hadn't moved.

"Come on, we can take a shower together."

"I'll be there in a minute," she said, her eyes still closed. Something was wrong. What was it? Ah, the condom. Why had he used it? He hadn't seemed to worry about it last night. She felt the chill penetrate her bones. He didn't want to take any chance they'd have a baby. He had made it clear a year ago he only wanted a temporary alliance. As he'd said last night, a baby would complicate things. Some of the warmth and glow of his lovemaking dimmed. She got up and followed him into the bathroom. She had always known where she stood with Cole. Nothing had changed.

And nothing had changed with their agreement. Maybe he'd stay for the three years, or maybe he'd be gone by the time his father and mother left on their cruise. In any event, she would still love him. Still want him.

The next three weeks were busy. Trisha finished her line edit and began her work for a new book. Her notebook accompanied her everywhere as she jotted ideas down. Some were personal, such as how she could entice Cole into trusting her enough to give himself permission to fall in love with her. Others were notations she made to follow up on finding out more facts to use in the book.

She thought her husband cared for her. He must; he could not be so generous a lover if he didn't. He'd made love to her almost every night. But was it enough? The patience she had counted on to carry her through was waning. She wanted to know, yet she was afraid to ask.

Matt came home. He had exercises to do, special foods to eat and biweekly checkups to pass. But he was steadily improving. While he tired easily and took a long nap every day, it was obvious to everyone he was on the road to full recovery.

Cole worked hard at Langford Construction, sometimes slipping back into the routine he'd followed in Kuwait of working as long as there was daylight. He had not told Trish of the change in ownership of the company, and she often wondered why.

Her tenants had found a new place and planned to move any day now, so her house would be available. On the day she found out, she drove to the Windmere site to tell Cole.

The construction had progressed a lot in the weeks since she'd visited. Several of the houses were enclosed, roofs were on most of them. Glaziers were working on two. But the office hadn't changed. Papers were still stacked in piles on both desks. Blueprints were pinned to the walls and on the drafting table. Yet there was a certain kind of order. Trisha suspected Cole knew where everything was.

He was on the phone when she pushed opened the door. The cool air was a welcome relief. The day was hot and she seemed to be bothered more and more by the humid summer heat. The short walk from her car had seemed interminable.

"Hi. What brought you by?" he said when he hung up the phone.

"Brought you some lunch. I heard from the Realtor this morning. My tenants will be moving out by the end of the week. They found a nice house in Larchmont and can move right away." She opened the bag and withdrew the thick roast beef sandwiches and chips. "I was hoping you'd have something cold to drink."

"Sodas are in the small refrigerator over there." He reached for one of the sandwiches. Opening the bag of chips, he shook some onto the paper plate. "So you'll be ready to move back home then," he said.

Trisha spun around, two cold sodas in her hand. She closed the refrigerator door with her hip, an odd pain piercing her heart at his comment.

"I guess I thought we'd both be moving into the house," she said carefully as she handed him a cold drink.

He raised his head to study her, his expression intent. "I don't know."

She fought the panic that threatened. "Might as well move in until your folks get ready for their cruise. They'd probably like some time alone, and there's time enough once they're gone to make up your mind. You'd be able to move back to their place while they were gone if you wanted to."

He nodded, slowly chewing his sandwich, his eyes never leaving hers. Trisha lowered her gaze, picked up a sandwich, wondering if she would be able to eat any of it. She was feeling slightly sick. What else could she say to make him decide to move in with her? She didn't want him to end their marriage. Not yet. Not ever.

"All right. We'll move at the end of the month. Take it from there," he agreed.

Her hand trembled as she raised a chip to her mouth. She was afraid to meet his gaze, for fear he'd see the relief in hers. She still felt shaky, and knew nothing had been resolved. But just as possession was nine-tenths of the law, so was proximity to love. Maybe he'd grow so used to having her around, he wouldn't want to change it.

"I'll arrange to have the furniture returned from storage. I thought of making the downstairs bedroom into an office. It's big enough for two desks—do you want me to get one for you?"

"Sure. I could do some of this paperwork at home if I had a place for it. Don't go spending much money, though."

She shook her head. "I won't." His warning was clear: don't spend a lot on something that might not last beyond six weeks.

"What are you doing this afternoon?" he asked, finishing the last of his lunch.

She shrugged. "Nothing much. I'm taking your mom to the grocery store later, while your dad naps."

He rose and moved to one of the windows. "Is she expecting you home soon?"

"No special time."

"Good." He snapped closed the blinds. Moving to the next window, he closed those, as well. The office grew dim as the sun's rays were shut out. He moved to the door and clicked the lock.

Anticipation crashed through Trisha as she watched him move around the room. She put the rest of her sandwich in the trash, stood to face him, her heart pounding, desire curling up inside.

"It's one thing," he began conversationally, "to try to make it through the day without you when I have plenty of work to do and few reminders of you." He stood right before her, his hands on her shoulders, drawing her closer and closer. "But it's quite another thing when you come calling." He kissed her.

"If I'm interrupting your work, I could leave," she said softly, tasting him with her lips and tongue.

"Not on your life." He lifted her and spun around to set her on the edge of the drawing table. Reaching around her, he swept the blueprints and notes off to the floor.

"Cole!"

"What?" He slid his hands up under her skirt, rubbing against her soft skin, teasing her with his kisses.

"On a drafting table?" Her mouth was never far from his. Her breath mingled with his as her hands began unbuttoning his work shirt, pushing it off his shoulders.

"It's sturdy enough, and—" he stopped to kiss her deeply "—it's going to be a lot easier to pick up the blueprints than it would be to—" he kissed her again "—pick up all the papers off my desk."

His hands gently tugged her panties down, dropping them on top of the blueprints. "Remember when you splashed whipped cream everywhere?" he asked, moving closer to her, his hands everywhere.

"Umm." She nodded.

"I discovered that day that your skin is as sweet without the cream." He opened his mouth on her shoulder, nipping softly, soothing with his tongue.

"Shouldn't you be working?" she asked, moving to snuggle even closer in his hard embrace.

"Even the boss deserves a lunch break," he said, unfastening his jeans.

Their lovemaking was wild, hot, quick. Trisha shivered in the aftermath, clinging to Cole with waning energy. He kissed her, holding her in his strong arms, soothing her, petting her as she gradually fell back to earth.

"I should bring lunch more often," she whispered in his ear.

"Come every day if you like," he replied.

She smiled at his pun and shook her head. Pushing back, she looked at him. His hair was tousled where her fingers had been. His eyes had the lazy satisfied look of a sated beast.

"Now I want a nap," she said as she unwound her legs from around his hips and strove for a bit of modesty. He yanked up his jeans, then helped her don her top, which he'd thrown across the room.

"So go to bed and think of me."

"That would keep me awake." Hopping off the table, she steadied herself against him. When he leaned over to kiss her again, she reached up eagerly for his embrace.

"I do have to go so you can get back to work," she said reluctantly, combing her fingers through her hair. Gathering up the remains of lunch, she glanced around, watching as Cole carefully tacked back the blueprints.

"This was probably a mistake," he grumbled.

She paused. Was he regretting—

"I'll never be able to use this drafting table again without seeing you on it," he said. "And, honey, you do a lot more for it than any blueprint ever did."

"I'll see you when you get home." She turned for the door.

"Trisha?"

Turning back, Trisha waited.

"Did you mention to Mom or Dad that we might be moving at the end of the month?"

"No, I wanted to tell you first."

"Hold off a day or so, will you? We can tell them together, later."

She swallowed hard. "Are you having second thoughts, Cole?"

He shook his head. "No. I just want to wait a couple of days, all right?"

She nodded and let herself out of the office. The heat and sun hit her the instant she closed the door behind her. But she didn't even notice the discomfort; she was too busy trying to understand why he would want to wait to tell his parents they were moving out.

The next afternoon Trisha stopped working on her book early and drove over to visit with Becky.

"This heat is wearing me out," Becky complained when they sat in the cool family room, large glasses of iced tea on the table before them.

"Me, too. I keep hoping for a series of thunderstorms just to cool things down," Trisha replied, leaning wearily against the sofa cushions. "For you, I'm sure it's worse—you have that baby in you to add to the discomfort."

"I know. Thank goodness it's only for another few weeks. Next time I'm going to plan to have the baby in the dead of winter!"

"Is there going to be a next time? Three kids is a bunch."

"I know, but Tom and I both love children. We're so happy doing things with Trevor and Tyler. If this one is another boy, I think we'll try one more time for a girl."

"And if it's a girl?"

"I don't know. I'd still like to have another one. We'll just have to see. So why aren't you and Cole starting a family?"

"Oh, you know. He wants to get the business going and all...." Trisha trailed off, wondering if what she suspected would change all that. She had to find out, if only for her own sake. "Do you mind that your dad gave Cole the family business?"

"Not at all. He divided it up into shares and I'll get some income from it, as long as Cole keeps it going. I never was interested in it. If I hadn't married Tom, I was going to be a nurse, remember?"

"Yes. Do you regret giving that up?"

"Not a bit. I love my family, love spending my time with the boys. And now that you're back, I'm complete. I missed you this past year. Is marriage with my brother all you thought it would be?"

"Of course, why wouldn't it be?" Trisha was guarded in her reply. Did Becky suspect things weren't perfect?

"I just wondered. You've loved him for so long, I wondered if the reality would match the dream."

"It's different," Trisha said.

Becky laughed and leaned over to squeeze her friend's hand. "I bet. Anyway, you're good for him. He deserves to have someone adore him, and you certainly have adored him forever."

"Is it so obvious?"

"Are you kidding? You've hidden it for years. If we hadn't been best friends, I would never have suspected. Even now you don't seem to fully relax around him. But he does know, doesn't he?"

"What husband doesn't know just how his wife feels?" Trisha asked, then changed the subject. She didn't want to go into all the details of her marriage, much as she longed to share the uncertainty and doubts she had. But she was married to Cole and owed him her first loyalty, even before her best friend.

But she wondered briefly if telling him she loved him would make any difference. She had been so careful to keep her feelings hidden. Was that a mistake? Should she have told him from the beginning?

Ten

Trisha tried to deny the envy she felt for her friend. Becky was so fortunate. She'd met Tom in college and they had both known they were right for each other. Marrying before Becky graduated, they had wasted no time in beginning their family. Soon their third child would be born into the love that surrounded each of their children.

Trisha sighed and pulled into the driveway. She cut the engine and leaned back. She was so tired she didn't even know if she could get into the house. With the air conditioner off, the Virginia heat began to seep into the car. Wearily she pushed open the door and headed for her room. She'd lie down, count her blessings and try to stamp out the envy that plagued her.

Why, she wondered as she sank gratefully back on the big queen-size bed, couldn't she and Cole have the same kind of love that Becky and Tom shared? These past three weeks had been blissfully happy ones for her. While she felt as if she were tiptoeing around on eggshells, she still had enjoyed a closer relationship to Cole than ever before.

Slowly her hand came to her stomach. If what she was beginning to suspect was true, how would that change things? Cole would make a wonderful father. Would he want to remain a husband, though?

She reached out for her pad. Darn, she'd left it down by her computer. She was too tired to get it, though. Nodding off to sleep, she made a mental note to add pregnancy test to her list of things to remember.

When Cole came home he was surprised to find Trisha sound asleep in their bed. He hesitated in the doorway. She'd never taken a nap that he'd known about in the year they'd been married. Was she coming down with something?

"Trisha?" He crossed the room to the edge of the bed, sitting beside her.

"Umm?" Slowly she opened her eyes, gazed at him for the longest moment without saying a word. Was she still sleeping, dreaming?

"Are you all right?" he asked.

She turned to look at the clock, her eyes widening in surprise at the lateness of the hour.

"Oh, gosh, I didn't mean to sleep for so long." Sitting up, she ran her fingers through her hair and shook her head as if to clear the traces of sleep that clung.

"How come you needed a nap?" He pushed his fingers into her hair, brushing it back from her face, letting the soft tangles entrap his hand, relishing the silky feel.

"I was just tired. This heat is getting to me."

"You've lived here all your life."

"I know. Maybe it's the humidity after the dry air in Kuwait. I'll be fine. Just needed a nap."

Cole waited, but she never met his eyes. Frowning in concern, he rose. "I need to shower. Are you sure everything is all right?"

"Why wouldn't it be?" she asked.

He watched her for another moment, then turned to get clean clothes to take in the bathroom with him.

"I'm fine, really. I'll go help your mom set the table," she said firmly.

Once he left the room, Trisha groaned and fell back against the pillows. She was still tired! She wanted to just roll over and go back to sleep and not wake up until morning. But she knew that would worry everyone. And there may be no reason for it.

Slowly she rose. She wanted to go splash some cold water on her face—maybe that would help. Brushing her hair, she pinched her cheeks to get some color and headed down toward the kitchen. There were only a few hours to get through before she could go back to sleep.

Detouring through the dining room, she picked up her pad and added a reminder about the pregnancy test. Not that she thought she'd have trouble remembering that, but habits were hard to break. She tossed the pad onto the table and headed toward the kitchen. Hearing a plop, she turned. The pad had slid off the table onto the carpet. She stared at it.

She was so tired she couldn't even think. Measuring the distance from the door to the far side of the table, she shook her head and turned back to the kitchen. She would pick it up later; right now she needed something to help her wake up. Maybe iced tea would help, or even iced coffee. Actually, bed was the only thing that would help.

Dinner was a strain. Cole watched her like a hawk. She drank several glasses of iced tea, but there was no punch from the caffeine. She still wanted to go back to bed. She had trouble following the conversation and a couple of times was asked by Peggy or Matt if she was feeling all right.

When the dishes were done, Trisha turned toward the backyard. They had taken to sitting outside in the evenings, enjoying the cooler air after the heat of the day. She had always been very fond of Becky's parents, but now she was getting to know them even better and loved them both.

"Dear, why don't you go on up to bed? You might be coming down with something and maybe a good night's sleep would nip it in the bud," Peggy suggested, coming up and putting her arm around Trisha's shoulders.

"It does sound good," Trisha said wistfully, watching Cole and his father laughing at some joke.

"Go on. We'll see you in the morning."

"I don't want Cole to worry."

"I'll tell him you're fine. Go on upstairs."

Sighing in defeat, Trisha nodded and turned. She walked through the dining room and picked up her pad. She knew she was exhausted when the effort to do so was almost more than she could stand. Carrying it upstairs, she put it on the dresser. Rummaging in the drawer, she found the sexy nightie she'd bought a few weeks ago. She and Cole had been sleeping without any clothes these past weeks. But for some reason she wanted to wear the nightgown tonight.

In less than ten minutes she was in bed. In less than one after that she was sound asleep.

Cole had left for work by the time Trisha awoke the next morning. She felt much better, refreshed and full of energy. Thank goodness all she'd needed was a good night's sleep.

Plot ideas and characterization traits were bubbling around in her mind as she sat down to her computer. The rest had definitely helped her creativity. The morning flew by as she typed page after page of the first chapter.

Trisha stretched and decided to take a break. It was lunchtime. She'd grab a bite to eat and make her trip to the drugstore before Peggy and Matt needed to leave for the weekly visit to his doctor. Nervous energy tingled inside. What would Cole say if she was pregnant? Would he be happy about it? They had never discussed children. He had questioned her that first night they made love. She had honestly thought she was safe. He'd been so careful to use a condom every other time they made love. No, not every time. In the office trailer at Windmere Site he hadn't. She closed her eyes, remembering every detail of the lunchtime visit. Smiling, she left for the store.

Shy about the entire situation, Trisha drove to a neighborhood where she didn't normally shop. She wasn't going to give rise to any gossip. If the test proved positive, she'd tell Cole first.

By the time she returned home, dark clouds were building on the horizon. Wind rustled the leaves on the trees. The signs of impending thunderstorms were everywhere. She hurried into the house.

"I'm not late, am I?" she asked as Peggy and Matt met her at the door.

"No. We thought we'd allow a bit extra time to drive. If it starts raining, we didn't want to feel rushed. I've left the windows open," Peggy said.

Trisha nodded. "I'll leave them that way until it actually begins to rain. Drive carefully."

The wind that blew the curtains into billowing clouds away from the windows would cool the house, clean the air. Time enough to shut that out when the rain came.

The phone rang; it was her agent. Trisha listened, blinking in shock. Slowly she took a deep breath. "Repeat that, Jack." When he complied, she let out a shriek and twirled around and around, getting tangled up in the phone cord.

"You did it! You pulled it off! I don't believe it," she shouted into the receiver. A major television network was going to use her books as the basis for a TV series. Her approval on scripts and casting was assured. It was the deal of a lifetime and Jack had pulled it off!

"What? Yes, yes, fax me the letter of intent. I want to read every single word. Oh, God, Jack, I can't believe it!"

After she finished the exciting call, she fairly flew across the room as the fax machine spewed the letter through. She eagerly read every line. Wait until she told Cole! Wait until Becky heard, she'd go bananas!

She looked at the telephone. No, she didn't want to tell Cole that way. She'd wait until he came home. And she had to tell him first. God, this was about the most exciting thing that had ever happened to her. She was delirious with happiness.

She smoothed out the fax copy of the letter and went upstairs to put it with her other writing correspondence. She kept all her records in one box—her royalty statements, contracts, agreement with her agent, all the papers related to her writing. Not very businesslike, but it suited her. Proudly she placed the latest letter on top.

She still had the small brown bag. Drawing out the pregnancy test kit, she opened it and read the instructions. She'd have to wait until morning. It seemed endless, but she didn't mind, not with the other news bubbling to be shared. Replacing the kit in the bag, she put it beneath the sink.

The wind was blowing harder than ever. Trisha went to the window and looked out across the backyard. The tree limbs moved in a swirling dance as their leaves fluttered beneath the unceasing breeze. She relished the coolness of the air. The thunderstorm would bring down the temperature. She, for one, would be glad of it.

Turning, she headed back downstairs for her computer, wondering if she would be able to write anything, or was she too excited to even think?

Cole pulled the truck to a stop. The car was gone. It was the middle of the afternoon. Didn't his father have a doctor's appointment today? He glanced again at the dark sky. The storm would hit in minutes. He had let everybody go home early. There'd be no working in a building site during a thunderstorm; it was too dangerous.

And, he hesitated to admit it, even to himself, he was anxious to see Trisha. He'd been worried about her last night. She'd still been sleeping when he left this morning. He hoped she wasn't getting sick.

When he walked into the kitchen, he could hear the click of her computer keys. Moving quietly to the connecting door, he watched her work. Her concentration was devoted to the screen before her as her fingers flew across the keyboard. She didn't know he was home.

Quietly he backed away and headed upstairs. He'd shower first, then let her know he was home.

The wind was blowing hard. The door to their room had been propped open, to keep it from slamming shut with the force of the wind. It felt good. It was time for the heat spell to break. Once the rain ended, everything would be fresh and clean and the air much cooler.

He drew out clean jeans, a shirt. The wind fluttered the pages of a pad, flipping them open, sliding the pad across the dresser.

Smiling, Cole reached out and smoothed down the pages. It was Trisha's notepad. She was always making lists. He picked it up. He'd place it—

His eyes caught the words and he paused, reading. He felt as if he'd been kicked in the gut. He dropped the clean clothes on the bed, sank down on the edge as he read the list.

"Get sexy nightie.... Verify joint checking.... Make Cole's favorite meals.... Mercedes vs. Maserati... Check insurance/inheritance... Pregnancy kit."

Pregnancy kit? His hand gripped the pad so tightly the cardboard bent. He'd been a damned fool. She was just like Diane. Just like all the women he'd ever known. He should have suspected. They had a very cool, distant relationship in Kuwait. When they returned home, when there was a distinct possibility his father wouldn't make it, suddenly

Trisha changed. Suddenly she was doing stripteases for him, flirting, doing all in her power to make him jealous with her talk of dating other men. Doing all in her power to ensnare him with emotions and sex until he had actually entertained thoughts about making their marriage permanent.

But she had never said she loved him. It had all been a carefully staged plan. She had even written everything down!

Rising, he went into the bathroom, glanced at the counter. Nothing. Opening the medicine cabinet, he saw nothing out of the ordinary. He opened the cupboard beneath the sink. Drawing out the brown bag, he took out the pregnancy kit.

Damn her! If she thought she could trap him into continuing this mockery of a marriage by getting pregnant, it was time she found out differently. If she thought now that he had the money and backing of Langford Construction she could latch on for a free ride, it was time he set her straight.

He took a deep breath. The rage that was building was like nothing he'd ever experienced. Even Diane's betrayal hadn't caused such anger.

He'd throw Trisha out on her ear so fast she wouldn't know what hit her. His father was recovered enough to stand the knowledge that Cole and Trisha were no longer a couple. Her house was vacant—she could move out today. He'd help her. He wanted her to be gone so he never had to see her again. She'd been contriving to change their marriage, all for the sake of a few lousy dollars. If his father had gone back to work, she'd have sung a different tune.

Slowly he turned and headed downstairs. He pushed open the door to his father's study and placed the kit and the pad in the center of the desk. He took a deep breath. It didn't soothe. He clenched his fists. He would not hurt her, though he longed to shake her until she cried for mercy. He would not rant and rage like he wanted to. He would call her in, demand an explanation about what he'd found and then get her the hell out of his life.

Deep inside, beneath the hot anger that threatened to swamp him, was a profound hurt. He had begun to trust her, had always cared for her. Now this. He didn't know how he would live the rest of his life knowing what she'd done. But he would.

He went to the dining room.

"Trisha, could I see you a moment?"

"Cole? Hi." Her smile was wide and open. Almost like the ones she gave to Becky. "I didn't know you were home..." she trailed off when she realized he was not smiling in return.

"In my father's study." He didn't know where his folks were, but he didn't want them barging in on this confrontation.

"Sure. Is something wrong?" Trisha got up and followed him into the study.

Cole closed the door, watching her. He saw her start when she saw the pregnancy test kit on the desk. And the pad. Had she thought he wouldn't ever discover her treachery?

"Oh," she said.

"Is that all you have to say? Oh?" He moved to the open window, hoping the breeze would cool him enough to deal with her rationally, calmly. He wanted to put his fist through something.

"I was going to tell you if the results were positive."

"Nice of you."

"You don't want a baby, I take it." Her voice sounded strained.

He swung around. "Did you think to trap me that way? You should have checked first."

"Trap you? What are you talking about?"

"Your great plan to trap me into the kind of marriage you wanted. Nice try, but no thanks."

"I don't know what you're talking about."

He crossed to the desk and picked up the notepad. "Let me read you some of your checklist for entrapment. Get sexy clothes, make favorite meals, sex games, pregnancy. You have check marks by some of these, but not all. You still haven't decided whether you want a Mercedes or a Maserati. You still don't know the inheritance situation, or the insurance." He tossed the pad back and glared at her. "And there is no need for you to know. This marriage is finished. I'm exercising my rights in the prenuptial agreement and ending it now. According to the agreement you signed a year ago, you get nothing. So all your efforts have blown up in your face."

God, he wanted to shake her until she begged his forgiveness. He wanted to take her upstairs and make love to her until she screamed for him, promised that she wanted only him and not his money or the things his money could buy.

She was staring at him as if he'd grown a second head.

"You're nuts. You are absolutely, certifiably nuts. That list is for my book."

"Fix Cole's favorite dinners is for your book?" he said in total disbelief.

"No. Some of it was personal. I need to jot things down to remember them. It's a habit. You know that."

"I know that for all the months we were in Kuwait you couldn't be bothered treating me any differently from the way you had the past few years. But the moment we arrived in Virginia, the moment you realized what a gold mine I would have if something happened to my father, everything changed. You saw me as your meal ticket for life and did all you could to latch on to that meal ticket with both hands."

"That's not true," she whispered, looking horrified.

"Of course it is, admit it. What about those sexy clothes you recently bought and wore with the intent of enticing me? It was damned hot in Kuwait, but you didn't buy new clothes there."

"Hardly. I was trying to behave with circumspection in an Arab country."

"Right. But you forgot I already went through this once, sweetheart. I know the drill. And I protected myself against you." When she backed up against the door, his temper flared. Striding over to her, he gripped her shoulders with hard hands.

"You can pack your bags and move out today. I'll make your excuses to my folks."

"Cole, listen to me. That list is about my story. Some of it was about you, but most of it is about my story."

She pushed against him, inflaming him even more. Without thinking, he crushed her against the door, his mouth coming down hard against hers. He pushed into her as if he sought oblivion in her embrace, as if he could forget all he'd discovered and recapture the happy moments he'd known with her.

She struggled, trying to push him away, but his mouth never eased its assault. Finally she was quiet. Slowly his kiss changed, from arrogant male dominance to that of a lover. His tongue tasted her, searched and discovered the hidden recesses of her mouth. Slowly his grip eased as the kiss went on and on.

He pulled back when he felt the tears against his cheeks.

She was crying, but she didn't look away. She glared at him as the tears traced their way down her cheeks. Her mouth was swollen and red. But her chin was tilted and she didn't move.

"You have me confused with Diane. I did not marry you for your money. I have never asked you for anything beyond the household expenses, which you said you wanted to provide. You arrogant jerk. You think money is so important?"

"It is to those who don't have it. Weren't you the one who told me all your father's insurance money had to go to his last illness? The income from Langford Construction must have looked mighty fine to you."

"Oh, you idiot. I have loved you since I was sixteen years old, and I don't have a clue why. You've never even seen me as a woman. You laughed at me when I was a teenager. I stayed away all these years because I couldn't bear it. I couldn't come to your wedding when you married someone else. I thought the happiest day of my life was the one when you asked me to marry you. But you are so warped by what happened with Diane that you can't see someone who loves you when they stand right before you. I would have done anything for you, and this is the way you treat me."

"Love, ha! Where was this great love while we were in Kuwait? Why am I only hearing about it now, when I've discovered your deception? We've been sharing the same bed for weeks, never a peep about love from you all this time. We've been *making love,* and never a peep. How much is this love worth—half my inheritance?" He glared at her, his anger fueled by her blatant attempt to claim love.

She knocked off the hands that still gripped her shoulders. "Wait right here, you self-righteous pig. Don't you move a muscle. I'll be right back!" She spun around and disappeared up the stairs.

Cole was breathing hard. He clenched his fists and glared at the furniture in the study. Sitting in the chair behind the desk, he glanced at the pad. He snatched it up and flung it across the room. He wished he'd never found the damn thing. He wished he was still living in some fairy-tale existence where he could wonder if marriage was in his future. If sharing his life with Trisha were a possibility.

He stared at the pregnancy kit, his thoughts spinning so fast he couldn't analyze how he felt. A baby. Were they really going to have a baby? Could he send her away if there was a baby? Who would take care of her? Of the baby?

The door slammed shut behind her. He looked up, struck with how beautiful she looked, even as furious as he. She had a sheaf of papers in her hand, and fiery anger in her eyes. Locking her gaze to his, she crossed the room to stand before the desk.

"You've ruined what could have been a wonderful day for me. You have probably ruined both our lives with your foul accusations and your inability to trust someone who loves you more than anything. You needn't worry about me anymore, Cole. I'll be gone before you know it. You didn't want me to love you when I was sixteen, and it's obvious you don't want my love even now. So be it."

"Trisha—"

"Shut up. I'm the one talking now. You had your say." She thumbed through the papers and withdrew one, slamming it down on the desk. "Here is my first contract. Please note the advance." Another paper followed.

"Here's my latest royalty statement. Please note the amount. I think it's fairly obvious I could buy anything I want."

Two more papers were slammed down before him. He couldn't even read the first one—she wasn't giving him a moment.

"Here are contracts two and three. Check out the escalation clauses."

She paused for breath, her gaze never returning to his, even though he gave up looking at the papers she kept slapping down on his desk and kept his eyes on her. He wanted to kiss her again. Her mouth was still swollen from his earlier kiss. He winced slightly. He really didn't want to hurt her, except to retaliate for her actions, her betrayal. For a moment he felt the prick of tears. Clenching his jaw, he looked up from her mouth. He hadn't cried since he was a boy—he sure as hell wasn't going to now.

"—going to tell you tonight. I thought you'd be so happy for me. Shows what a lousy judge of character I am."

He blinked, glanced at the latest document she threw down. "What is it?"

"The result of weeks of negotiations. My book is going to be the basis for a weekly TV series. Trust me, Cole, your money is the last thing in this world I need. I'll make so much off this I won't be able to spend it all. So take your precious construction company and all the money you make from it and enjoy it in your old age. The baby and I don't need you."

Tears were running down her cheeks, but she still glared at him. Snatching up the pregnancy test kit, she stormed out of the room, slamming the door behind her again.

Cole felt as if a whirlwind had swept through. He glanced down at the letter on top of the pile of papers she'd delivered. Reading it through, he shook his head. She was going to make a fortune with this deal. Slowly he picked up the next one, read it. Read them all.

Rain started falling and he got up to shut the window, all but an inch or two. He still needed the cooling air to cool his temper.

He continued reading, studied the royalty statements. She'd included her bank statement. While she couldn't buy and sell him today, she came close to it. All this time he thought he was supporting her, and she had enough money after the first royalty check to live comfortably for a long, long time.

"I've loved you since I was sixteen years old." He leaned back in the chair. "Hell," he said. If it were true, he'd probably succeeded in his wish to hurt her as much as he was hurting. He should have asked for an explanation, not jumped right in on her. He should have known better. He'd known her for years. He had lived with her. Trisha was nothing like Diane, or the others. Dammit, he *knew* that. How could he have thought otherwise for even a minute?

Slowly Cole rose, his anger gone. He would apologize, explain why he had thought what he'd thought. She would understand. She had to. He opened the study door. The wind was blowing rain in through his mother's windows.

Quickly he went around the ground floor, closing windows, wiping up the rain. He went upstairs. Their door was wide open. The rain blew in across the floor, reaching the bed. The window hadn't been closed. He slammed it shut and looked around. Where was Trisha? She hadn't been downstairs. He thought she was up here.

He looked across the hall. The bathroom door was open.

For the second time that day he felt as if he'd been kicked. She was gone. Where? He looked out the window. It was pouring. Lightning flashed and a short time later the harsh crack of thunder shattered the afternoon.

He crossed to the guest room in the front of the house and looked out. The truck was still there. Where had she gone in this downpour?

He went back to the study, called his sister. A few minutes later, he hung up. Trisha wasn't there, but Becky would call him if she arrived. Staring out at the thunderstorm, he hoped she wasn't walking in it. Maybe she'd gone to one of the neighbors. Truly worried now, he reached for the phone and began searching for his wife.

Eleven

Cole pulled into the driveway. Cutting the lights and engine, he climbed out, carrying a small package. The storm had blown itself out, the air was fresh and clean. It was twilight, the last of the stormy afternoon fading into darkness as the clouds dissipated. He heard the buzz of the cicadas as they began their nightly song. The air had cooled, yet it was still warm.

Mounting the shallow steps to the wide porch, he wondered if she were here. He didn't know where else to look, he'd already tried every place he could think of. His expression wavered between anger and determination, uncertainty and hope. The entire afternoon had been hell. Had he lost everything? Lost his wife, a family, a future?

Reaching the front door, he peered through the glass oval into the dark, empty house. No lights anywhere. Damn, she had to be here.

He had to find her. He needed to talk to her, get his life back on track. For a moment fear touched him. *If* he could get his life back on track.

Walking around to the back of the house, he spotted her. She was sitting on the big porch swing, alone, in the dark. For a moment he remembered finding her like this a year ago. Just after her father had died. The night he'd come to make his pitch. Skirting one of the many islands of flowers in the green yard, he approached her, waiting for her to notice him. He could smell the honeysuckle that clung to the back fence, the sweet scent adding to the reminiscences of that night a year ago. She'd been sad then, too.

"Trisha?"

She looked up listlessly. "Cole? What are you doing here?"

In three strides he joined her on the swing, sank down beside her. She'd been crying. He could see it on her face and in the damp handkerchief she clutched in her hand. Her dress was rumpled, her feet tucked up beneath the skirt. For a second something twisted deep within him. He'd caused this anguish. He hoped he could end it.

"I had to find you," he said softly. Without thinking about it, he reached out and drew her up against him, praying she wouldn't resist.

Tricia held herself stiffly until, unable to resist, she gradually relaxed against him as his hand gently rubbed her back. He said nothing. She remained silent.

For over a decade he'd thought of her almost as a sister. Once again he remembered the day she met him. He let himself remember the weeks that followed when she had revealed the crush she had on him. Only she had called it love. For eleven years, she had called it love. And he had once again thrown it back into her face.

"I'm sorry." His voice was low. He wanted to say more, but the words wouldn't come. Slowly he brushed his fingers against her arm, feeling the satin heat beneath him. She remained silent. Had he ruined it? Had he been too slow in learning the truth to save his marriage, which he now knew he wanted more than anything in the world?

He tried to think how to bring up the subject uppermost in his mind without sounding crass and insensitive. His heart pounded. There was no delaying.

"When will you use the pregnancy kit?" he asked finally.

Trisha shrugged. "In the morning. Don't worry, I won't be a burden."

He closed his eyes at her words, the pain piercing his heart.

"You never have been. I never thought you would be."

She stirred and pulled away. He pushed them back and forth on the swing, frustration sizzling through as she rejected his touch.

"Trish, I have an idea I want you to seriously consider," he began hesitantly. He needed her to say yes. He needed to present it properly, to make sure he gave her no reason to refuse. She had to listen to him!

"Not this time, Cole. You had an idea last year and look where it got me. I should have refused you then. I, too, have learned something over the year."

He closed his eyes, then snapped them open. The sky was black, the stars scattered across like brilliant diamonds. He sighed. It wouldn't be easy. But he'd had a lot of time to think after she'd left this afternoon. Now he had to make things right. If he ever wanted a moment of peace and happiness, he had to make things right.

"I'm not very good at this," he said.

"Go home, Cole. There's nothing left to talk about. You were very clear in your opinion and feelings this afternoon."

"No. I have to say a few things. Then I'll leave." He hoped to God he wouldn't be leaving, but that was up to Trisha.

"What?"

He took a deep breath. Her tone didn't sound very promising, but then he couldn't blame her after all he'd said that afternoon.

"We met when you were sixteen and I was twenty."

She crossed her arms and stared out over the gray yard.

"So you didn't know me in high school."

"If we're here to rehash old days—"

"Hear me out, Trisha, that's all I want." Not everything, but all he had a right to for the time being. "When I was a junior I made quarterback on the football team. That same fall I met Sara Carter. She was the prettiest thing I'd seen up to that point. We started dating and soon were going steady. Late in the fall of my senior year I pulled a shoulder muscle pretty badly. It looked as if I wouldn't be able to play in any more games. That's when Sara discovered she really didn't love me. She was attracted to the quarterback who could still play ball and garner the adulation of the other students."

Cole was watching Trisha. He saw her turn to look at him.

"You know about Diane, now you know about Sara. There was a girl in college, too, who wanted what I had to offer, more than me." He shook his head. "Do you wonder with my track record that I'm not more trusting around women? Even around women who I know are different?"

"I guess not," she said softly.

"Here, this is for you." He thrust the wrapped parcel into her lap. "I was kind of hoping you'd wear it whenever I get bent out of shape and start throwing accusations." He hoped she'd be around when he got bent out of shape the next time. He hoped he hadn't ruined their lives, as she'd said earlier.

Trisha lifted the package, slid a finger beneath the taped end and ripped the paper. She withdrew a T-shirt. Holding it before her, she could tell it had something on the front. "A shirt?" she asked.

"Yes. I had it specially made."

"It's too dark to see it."

"It says 'I am *not* Diane,' emphasis on the not."

Trisha crushed the shirt to her, closing her eyes against the surge of emotions that swept through her. Why was he here? What did he really want? Dared she let herself hope he'd changed his mind? She looked at him, wishing they had light, wishing she could know what he was thinking.

She cleared her throat. "So I'm to wear this—"

"The next time I behave like a total idiot. Trisha, I don't want to end our marriage. I want to be with you tomorrow when you take that pregnancy test. If you're pregnant, I want to know as soon as you do. Hell, honey baby, I want you like I've never wanted anyone else. I'm sorry for my temper this afternoon, sorry for the harsh things I said. Don't leave, Trisha, stay with me and make our marriage work."

Time stood still. The star-sprinkled sky gave no answer when she searched it. Trisha didn't know what to say. She longed to agree to stay with him, but doubt and hurt made her hesitate. What about the next time something set him off? She smiled slowly; she could always wear the T-shirt.

"Trisha?"

"I don't know, Cole," she began.

He exhaled as if he'd been holding his breath and reached out to draw her into his lap, settling her against his chest, his arms locked firmly around her. "Tell me you don't love me anymore, tell me you lied about loving me since you were sixteen, and I'll get up and leave. I won't contest any divorce, and if you're pregnant, I'll set up a trust for the baby. But if you can't tell me all that, then I'm not going anywhere."

Stalling for time, hoping she would think up the right thing to say, she traced her fingers across his shoulder, liking the strength she felt beneath the cotton, longing to touch his bare skin, to have him touch her. "I thought you only wanted a temporary marriage."

"A year ago that's what I thought, too. Now I want forever."

"Why?" She felt so cherished being held in his arms. Her head rested on his shoulder and she closed her eyes as he spoke. She had always loved his voice. As much as she loved every other aspect of Cole Langford.

"Did you know I was secretly flattered that you had that crush on me when we first met?"

"Right. You showed me how you felt." Even now, a decade later, she felt the sting of rejection at his mocking laughter.

"No, I showed you how an arrogant boy shows off to his peer group, too afraid to let his real feelings show, lest he be the butt of ridicule. I was flattered. If you hadn't suddenly started acting like I was poison, I might have asked you out."

"I overheard you and some of your friends laughing at me. Of course I stayed away," she said slowly.

"Honey baby, I'm sorry." He rested his cheek on her hair.

The blood roared through her veins, her heart pounded. She couldn't hide her feelings around this man. She had loved him as long as she'd known him—nothing had changed. All the anger and harsh words in the world wouldn't change her.

"You don't need to be tied to me. And if I'm pregnant, you can still see the baby."

He tipped up her chin. Trisha could just catch the gleam in his eyes as he rubbed a thumb over her lips. "I love you, Trisha. I realized that today. That was part of the reason I was so angry. I felt more betrayed than I ever felt with Diane. I thought a part of me had been ripped out and trampled. When you left, when I couldn't find you, I knew then what my life would be like if our marriage ended. I couldn't imagine living until Christmas without you, much less the rest of my life. Say you'll forgive me for my harsh words today. Tell me you love me enough to give me another chance. I will cherish you until I die. Don't let today's mistake keep us apart.''

"Oh, Cole, I love you so much I ache with it." She wanted to tell him how much he'd always meant to her, but his mouth covered hers and she was lost.

His hands roamed over her, rubbing gently against the soft skin of her shoulder, slipping down the strap to bare more for his kisses. He trailed down her throat, sipping at the sweet nectar as he traced her collarbone, dipped even lower. Trisha gave herself up to the lovemaking, her heart swelling with joy. It was better than anything she'd ever known. They had made love before, but she'd had to guard her true feelings. Now she could allow them free rein.

He raised his head as she unbuttoned his shirt and pushed it off his shoulders. "Probably not a bed in the house," he grumbled, gently nipping her earlobe.

She shook her head. "No, but there's plenty of grass." She wanted to be closer, so close they were one. She was on fire for him, desperate to show how much she loved him.

"It's wet."

"So what? Come on." Trisha stood up and pulled him up with her. In three steps they were in the thick grass beside the house. Trisha spread out the new T-shirt, then skimmed her sundress down over her hips.

"You are so beautiful." Cole reached out a finger to trace the swell of her breasts, circling the taut peaks, touching lightly.

"Umm, hurry up." She reached for his belt buckle, her fingers almost too numb to work. Heat and excitement shimmered through her as he quickly shed his clothes and drew her down to the makeshift bed.

"Hurry," she urged him.

He held off. "You never said if we were staying married." His fingers caressed her inner thigh, coming to rest in the damp curls at their apex.

"Yes."

"Yes, what, sweetheart?" One finger slipped inside. She was hot and wet and ready for him. He could hardly stand the wait, but he wanted to make sure everything was agreed. Time enough later to work out all the details, like ripping up the prenuptial agreement, choosing a weekend to spend at Virginia Beach and deciding how many children to have.

"Yes, I want to stay married. But even more right now I want you inside me!"

"Just to show you what a wonderful husband I'm going to be, I'll oblige you." He spread her legs and slid into the honey-hot warmth of her body. Closing his eyes as the exquisite pleasure built to fiery heights, he knew he would never regret this moment. He loved Trisha, and she loved him. It was all he needed.

Epilogue

"Trisha?"

"I'm upstairs," she called back, rocking the baby gently. He was just about asleep. His tummy full, he was no longer sucking, just mouthing her nipple. In a moment he'd drop off and she'd put him to bed.

"What— Oh, is he sleeping?" Cole came quietly into the bright, cheerful nursery.

"Almost. What did you need?"

He grinned and leaned over to kiss her softly. "I need you." He kissed her again, his fingertips trailing down across her exposed breast. "You're still the prettiest thing I ever saw."

"I thought that was Sara What's-her-name," Trisha said against his mouth, leaning forward for another kiss.

He stood up and gently took the now-sleeping baby from her. "That was in high school. My standards have risen since then. You now rank as the prettiest thing I've ever seen. Especially when holding Matthew."

Trisha smiled at the compliment. The past year had been wonderful. She knew she had never been happier.

"What did you want?" She joined Cole as he laid the baby in the crib, covering him lightly. Matthew was growing so fast he'd soon be able to sit up by himself. Then he'd be walking, and who knew what kind of mischief he'd get into?

"Did the mail come?" she asked, leaning against him as she watched their son settle down.

"Yes, and you got a ton of stuff. There's an envelope from your agent. Looks like maybe line edits on the latest book. Then there's a packet from the studio. Do you have more scripts to approve?"

"I don't know. I thought I was caught up. I'll have to see. Is that why you called me?"

Cole put his arm around her shoulder and walked her from the nursery. Turning down the hall to their room, he didn't stop until they were inside. "Actually, I came to ask you something, but now that I know Matthew's asleep and we have a few hours before we go to dinner at Becky's, I've thought of something better to do."

"Better than what?" She smiled as he drew his shirt over his head and threw it across the room. The familiar tug of excitement and anticipation began to build. She still hadn't outgrown the shimmering waves of awareness that flooded her body any time she was near this sexy man. She began to unbutton her top.

"Better than working on the mower. Which is why I called you. I found the T-shirt I bought you in the rag pile."

She nodded, slipping the shorts down her legs and kicking them away. When she was naked, she turned and saucily walked over to the bed, glancing at him over her shoulder in what she hoped was a most provocative manner. His desire for her became more evident by the second.

"I don't need it anymore," she said, drawing back the spread.

He picked her up and spun them both around twice before falling back on the mattress, still holding her in his arms. "Why is that?" He kissed her.

When she could speak again, Trisha snuggled up against her husband.

"The reason I no longer need my T-shirt is that I am totally convinced that you love me. I don't want any reminders of the past—it's gone and forgotten. I only want the shining future that you offer me."

"Ah, honey baby, I love you."

*   *   *   *   *

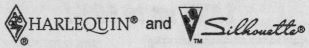

HARLEQUIN® and **Silhouette®**

are proud to present...

HERE COME THE GROOMS™

Four marriage-minded stories written by top Harlequin and Silhouette authors!

Next month, you'll find:

A Practical Marriage	by Dallas Schulze
Marry Sunshine	by Anne McAllister
The Cowboy and the Chauffeur	by Elizabeth August
McConnell's Bride	by Naomi Horton

ADDED BONUS! In every edition of *Here Come the Grooms* you'll find $5.00 worth of coupons good for Harlequin and Silhouette products.

On sale at your favorite Harlequin and Silhouette retail outlet.

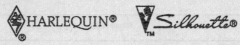

HARLEQUIN® **Silhouette®**

HCTG896

Look us up on-line at: http://www.romance.net

SAVE *up to 50%!*

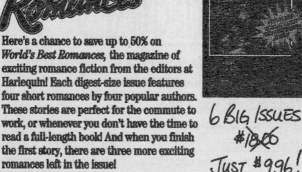

FORTUNE'S Children™

Bestselling Author
LISA JACKSON

Continues the twelve-book series—FORTUNE'S CHILDREN
in August 1996 with Book Two

THE MILLIONAIRE AND THE COWGIRL

When playboy millionaire Kyle Fortune inherited a Wyoming
ranch from his grandmother, he never expected to come
face-to-face with Samantha Rawlings, the willful woman
he'd never forgotten...and the daughter he'd never known.
Although Kyle enjoyed his jet-setting life-style, Samantha and
Caitlyn made him yearn for hearth and home.

MEET THE FORTUNES—a family whose legacy is greater than
riches. Because where there's a will...there's a *wedding!*

*A CASTING CALL TO
ALL FORTUNE'S CHILDREN FANS!*
If you are truly one of the fortunate
few, you may win a trip to
Los Angeles to audition for
Wheel of Fortune®. Look for
details in all retail Fortune's Children titles!

You can run, but you cannot
hide...from love.

OUTLAWS
and
Lovers

This August, experience danger, excitement and
love on the run with three couples thrown
together by life-threatening circumstances.

Enjoy three complete stories by some of your
favorite authors—all in one special collection!

THE PRINCESS AND THE PEA
by Kathleen Korbel

IN SAFEKEEPING
by Naomi Horton

FUGITIVE
by Emilie Richards

Available this August wherever books are sold.

Silhouette®

The exciting new cross-line continuity series about love, marriage—and Daddy's unexpected need for a baby carriage!

It all began with *THE BABY NOTION*
by Dixie Browning (Desire #1011 7/96)

And the romance in New Hope, Texas, continues with:

BABY IN A BASKET
by Helen R. Myers (Romance #1169 8/96)

Confirmed bachelor Mitch McCord finds a baby on his doorstep and turns to lovely gal-next-door Jenny Stevens for some lessons in fatherhood—and love!

Don't miss the upcoming books in this wonderful series:

MARRIED...WITH TWINS!
by Jennifer Mikels (Special Edition#1054, 9/96)

HOW TO HOOK A HUSBAND (AND A BABY)
by Carolyn Zane (Yours Truly #29, 10/96)

DISCOVERED: DADDY
by Marilyn Pappano (Intimate Moments #746, 11/96)

DADDY KNOWS LAST continues
each month...only from

Silhouette®

DKL-R

As seen on TV!
Free Gift Offer

With a Free Gift proof-of-purchase from any Silhouette® book,
you can receive a beautiful cubic zirconia pendant.

This gorgeous marquise-shaped stone is a genuine cubic
zirconia—accented by an 18" gold tone necklace.

(Approximate retail value $19.95)

Send for yours today...

compliments of 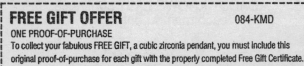 *Silhouette*®

To receive your free gift, a cubic zirconia pendant, send us one original proof-of-purchase, photocopies not accepted, from the back of any Silhouette Romance™, Silhouette Desire®, Silhouette Special Edition®, Silhouette Intimate Moments® or Silhouette Yours Truly™ title available in August, September or October at your favorite retail outlet, together with the Free Gift Certificate, plus a check or money order for $1.65 U.S./$2.15 CAN. (do not send cash) to cover postage and handling, payable to Silhouette Free Gift Offer. We will send you the specified gift. Allow 6 to 8 weeks for delivery. Offer good until October 31, 1996 or while quantities last. Offer valid in the U.S. and Canada only.

Free Gift Certificate

Name: _____

Address: _____

City: _____ State/Province: _____ Zip/Postal Code: _____

Mail this certificate, one proof-of-purchase and a check or money order for postage and handling to: SILHOUETTE FREE GIFT OFFER 1996. In the U.S.: 3010 Walden Avenue, P.O. Box 9077, Buffalo NY 14269-9077. In Canada: P.O. Box 613, Fort Erie, Ontario L2Z 5X3.

FREE GIFT OFFER
084-KMD

ONE PROOF-OF-PURCHASE

To collect your fabulous FREE GIFT, a cubic zirconia pendant, you must include this original proof-of-purchase for each gift with the properly completed Free Gift Certificate.

084-KMD